The Montana Vigilantes

The Montana Vigilantes

Tom Curry

WHEELER
CHIVERS

This Large Print edition is published by Wheeler Publishing, Waterville, Maine, USA and by BBC Audiobooks Ltd, Bath, England.

Wheeler Publishing is an imprint of Thomson Gale, a part of The Thomson Corporation.

Wheeler is a trademark and used herein under license.

LIBRARY OF CONGRESS CATALOGING-IN-PUBLICATION DATA

Curry, Tom, 1900–
  The Montana vigilantes / by Tom Curry.
    p. cm. — (A Rio Kid western series) (Wheeler Publishing large print western)
    ISBN-13: 978-1-59722-512-0 (softcover : alk. paper)
    ISBN-10: 1-59722-512-6 (softcover : alk. paper)
    1. United States — History — Civil War, 1861–1865 — Fiction. 2. Large type books. I. Title.
  PS3505.U9725M66 2007
  813'.52—dc22   2007002395

BRITISH LIBRARY CATALOGUING-IN-PUBLICATION DATA AVAILABLE

Published in 2007 in the U.S. by arrangement with
Golden West Literary Agency.
Published in 2007 in the U.K. by arrangement with
Golden West Literary Agency.

U.K. Hardcover: 978 1 405 64108 1 (Chivers Large Print)
U.K. Softcover: 978 1 405 64109 8 (Camden Large Print)

Printed in the United States of America on permanent paper
10 9 8 7 6 5 4 3 2 1

The Montana Vigilantes

CHAPTER I
GETTYSBURG

The guns had been roaring through nightmare hours which had stretched to interminable days. They shook the earth on which stood the little Pennsylvania town of Gettysburg, near which General Meade had joined in battle with the great Confederate General Robert E. Lee, who was making his supreme bid for victory by his invasion of the North to outflank Washington.

The largest armies ever before maneuvered were fighting savagely for mastery in this greatest battle, in July, 1863. Heroes in butternut gray and men in Union blue, brother fighting brother in that most horrible of all conflicts, civil war, were giving their lives as their blood stained the rich, warm fields of Gettysburg.

Back and forth the great battle raged, first one side and then the other seizing the advantage. Round Top, Little Round Top, Seminary Ridge. . . .

Miles to the west, General George A. Custer, General Phil Sheridan's brilliant and successful brigadier, led a surprise charge on the flower of the Confederate cavalry, the raiders of Jeb Stuart. Custer struck as Stuart was making ready one of his shrewd and theretofore highly successful encircling movements, meaning to ride around behind the enemy and cut off communications.

The dashing, smiling Custer, a striking, broadshouldered figure in his army blue, with the wide yellow cavalry stripe down his long legs and a curved Stetson strapped on his handsome, leonine head, raised his saber and the sunlight glinted on the sheening blade. The Fifth Michigan Cavalry he commanded was a raw organization but where Custer went, men would follow.

They broke from the trees and swept across a meadow toward the woods where one of Custer's trusted scouts, Captain Robert Pryor, had just reported that the Confederates were making up their ranks.

Pryor rode close to his commander, for whom he would willingly die. Down on the Rio Grande, where Bob Pryor had been born, he was known as the "Rio Kid," a happy-go-lucky cowboy, but here he was a full captain in the Grand Army, and a valuable scout for Custer, undertaking the most dangerous of missions with a nonchalance that accented his bravery.

In his blue eyes shone a devil-may-care light that spoke of reckless courage. His bronzed cheeks glowed with the health of youth, small lines at the corners of his generous mouth showed how quick he was to laugh, and his crisp, chestnut hair was cropped short.

Broad at the shoulders, he tapered to a narrow waist that was circled by a three-inch-wide sword belt which carried his Army pistols and saber. He was the ideal weight and height for a cavalryman and though just past twenty, he had a veteran's detachment in battle. Having ridden before he could walk, as was so often the case with boys down at his home on the Rio Grande, the Rio Kid was more at ease on horseback than afoot.

His passion for neatness was a splendid asset in the Army; aways he kept his gear and arms in meticulous order. But also about him was the air of a man born to command, of efficiency, that was impressive.

A heart-breaking choice had been forced upon the Rio Kid at the beginning of the Civil War, for it had been necessary for him to decide whether he would fight for the Union or for his own state. That experience had come to millions of men, but Bob Pryor had made his choice and was giving his best whole-heartedly to the Union.

Under him as he galloped close to George A. Custer was a young mustang, Saber, a horse that long since had become far more to him than just a mount. Saber was lanky and down his ridgy backbone ran a black stripe, for he was of the "breed that never dies." He had one mirled eye, with white and blue streaks shot through the iris. And he rolled that eye now, snorting as he charged. Saber loved a fight, and would dash into the thickest of gunfire, if allowed.

The earth shook with the thunder of hoofs. From the woods came the shrill "Rebel" yell.

"There's a wagon road through on the left sir," the Rio Kid called to Custer, as they rode.

Custer hit the wagon road, with the Rio Kid at his side, as the Fifth Michigan charged into the woods. Bullets were snapping through the leaves, hitting men behind them, but the Rio Kid and his great commander seemed to bear charmed lives.

Stuart's men were not yet in battle formation, and the surprise attack caught them dismounted. Confusion resulted, but the Southerners and Union men alike fought with a cool ferocity, the bravest of the bravest pitted against one another.

Sabers flashed silver, then red; pistols roared. The clash as the lines met was deafening. Hoarse shouts of men at war, the screeching of wounded horses, the cries of injured filled the woods.

Custer's charge carried him a mile through the enemy's left flank, while knots of fighting men were still at it in the woods.

"Captain," he ordered Bob Pryor, putting in his sweat-lathered black charger, "I want you to take a message back to General Sheridan. Hurry it."

"Yes, sir."

The Rio Kid waited while Custer hastily scrawled a report. He took it and rode, not back the way they had come, but on an angle that was the most direct route to headquarters. It took him dangerously close to enemy groups, and bullets were like swarming bees around about him.

He rode fast on a narrow path through the trees and brush, low over the swift dun. The Rio Kid knew the importance of the message he carried for Custer. Sheridan must know how far they had penetrated and the condition of the vital flank, so that in

11

turn he could report to General Meade, Commander-in-Chief of the Union Army at Gettysburg.

The long-legged, rangy dun had just flashed into a natural clearing in the forest when the Rio Kid caught a glimpse of a man in a torn gray uniform, and with black-beard stubble on his bullet head, bending over a limp gray-clad figure. Pryor saw the bending man take a black leather wallet and a turnip-sized gold watch from the senseless Confederate officer's pocket.

But Pryor had seen plenty of looters in both armies. He knew their cruel, sly ways. Instead of fighting, they would feign a wound or sneak off, and keep out of danger. Then they would rob the dead or seriously wounded. Both sides hated such despicable misfits, and the penalty was death if one was caught.

This time the victim was a man with a gray chin beard and a bronzed, well shaped forehead. He wore a brigadier-general's insignia, and blood was oozing from his chest, through his torn tunic. As the Rio Kid swerved, hand dropping to his pistol, the Confederate officer aroused, perhaps stirred by the looter.

"Stop it, you thief —" he mumbled.

A pistol was lying on the ground, close to

12

the looter's hand. With a curse and snarl, he seized it and aimed at the general's face.

The Rio Kid fired a breath before the looter. The man gave a sharp cry of alarm, dropped what he had been attempting to steal, and leaped away. On his face was a twisted snarl, and black eyes were flashing hate as he fired twice at Pryor. The looter had only been grazed, for Pryor's snapshot from horseback, to save the life of the Confederate officer, had been hurried.

But as the Rio Kid felt the sting of lead that touched his bronzed cheek and drew blood, when the looter shot at him, he fired again. And this time his bullet drove into the thief's ribs and to the heart. The looter crashed dead in the brush.

The Confederate general looked up at the man in blue. "Thank yuh — suh," he gasped. "Yuh have saved me, Captain."

The wounded man needed water — the Rio Kid could see that. But with his important mission, there was no time to stop. However, he did quickly dismount and give his own canteen to the man in gray.

"Yuh'll be picked up pronto, suh," he said. "By our side or yores. I'll send a stretcher for yuh as soon as possible. What's yore name?"

"General David Roberts — of Jeb Stuart's

command." The calm brown eyes fixed the strong face of the Rio Kid. "And you —"

A shrill Rebel yell close at hand told the Rio Kid he must not loiter. Gray-clad men were coming from the woods.

He hit leather and spurred off, followed by bullets. But he was satisfied that General Roberts would be safe now. . . .

Captain Bob Pryor found General Sheridan sitting his bay horse by the headquarters tent on a little hill, field-glasses in hand. The great general, he thought, would have been recognized anywhere, for there was no mistaking that round, bullet head, with the short hair standing out at right angles to his hat brim, nor the imperial and mustache. But his short-legged, long-bodied figure sat his horse like a centaur.

Sheridan was frowning, as the Rio Kid stopped beside him. His weatherbeaten face showed his anxiety. He could not permit Stuart to flank him. That would mean ruin for Meade, perhaps the end of the war, with victory for the South.

Saluting, Bob Pryor presented the message from Custer. Sheridan's lobster-hued face cleared as he read the hasty report. He looked around sharply.

"Major Yates — Captain de Forrest" — he began to tell off aides-de-camp, then paused, fixing the Rio Kid with his shrewd eyes. "And you, Captain," he said. "Pryor, isn't it?"

"Yes, sir."

"I have three identical messages to go to General Meade's headquarters, instantly. They mean life or death, and one of you three must get them to their destinations. Hurry."

The next minute the Rio Kid was riding toward the booming guns of Gettysburg, carrying Sheridan's message — the message that would tell Meade his right flank was safe.

A pall of smoke and red haze hung over the terrible field of battle. Woods that not long before had been stately, leafy trees were now only rows of black, smashed stumps. The ground was full of pits — shallow trenches dug by both sides in hasty entrenchment.

Puffs of gunsmoke showed from rocks and hills, and the heavier guns made a bass accompaniment to the rattle of muskets. Long lines of gray over there, lines of blue here. They spread before the Rio Kid's eyes as he crossed the corner of the great battlefield.

The ridges were held by fighting men. Groups swirled in mad engagements, man to man. Bayonets were bloody, pistols were fired pointblank, as back and forth the tide of the long battle rolled.

As the Rio Kid, dodging lead, galloped the fast dun on, heading for General George Gordon Meade's headquarters that were set back from the lines, he could see a mile ahead to where bayonets that resembled nothing so much as a moving picket fence, started straight up a hill at strongly entrenched Union forces. He caught his breath hard as he watched the magnificent charge.

Never wavering, straight into the mouths of the Union cannon, keeping ranks, the veterans advanced. And Bob Pryor recognized those men! While doing reconnaissance for Custer, he had come to know the more famous of the Southern regiments.

"Those are Pickett's men," he muttered.

But he did not slow or stop, even as he saw the wonderful fighting men of Pickett's regiment throw themselves against certain death. His own duty was to get that report of Sheridan's to General Meade. But as he galloped on he saw wide holes ripped in the gray ranks by grapeshot, as the Union soldiers, down behind a barricade, decimated them.

It was impossible, that charge — or Pickett would have made it!

The whole field was a scene of carnage. It

16

was covered with dead or dying soldiers and horses, overturned, smashed wagons, and the gear of the dead and dying. For moments, as he sped on, the Rio Kid closed his eyes to the awful sight.

As he approached General Meade's headquarters, he saw that the general was standing outside, grimly watching the battle. The Rio Kid was the first of the three aides to reach his side. Pryor was the trim young officer he always was as he drew himself up stiffly, with only a slight trace of blood on one cheek to show that he had but recently done battle himself.

Meade's eyes lighted as he read Sheridan's report. Hastily he wrote a congratulatory message to his cavalry general.

"This isn't vital, Captain," he told Pryor, and his whole tall, burly figure vibrated with relief. "Ride around the long way, if you wish."

"Yes, General."

The Rio Kid saluted, and even as he turned the dun he saw that Yates and de Forrest were in sight, bringing copies of Sheridan's note. For once, a general would receive three identical messages, but as usual, no chances had been taken. Odds were always three to one that one man would arrive with an important missive.

17

Anxious to see what had happened to Pickett on that foredoomed charge, the Rio Kid returned the way he had come. His blood chilled as he saw that half the men in gray who had so valiantly charged up that slope now lay there, dead or wounded. The other half, still undaunted, had coolly reformed, to charge again.

"War!" the Rio Kid cried to high heaven, as the red haze of battle swirled about him. "It's inferno!"

He had started to ride on when a young officer, a lieutenant by his insignia, came riding swiftly up from the flank. He had been in the fight and had received a wound, which had been dressed. Now he was plunging back in.

"Hot today, Lieutenant!" Pryor called.

"Yes, Captain. . . . Why, hello, Captain Pryor! I didn't recognize you. I'm Adam Byrne, of the Third Pennsylvania. Remember me? We met at Sheridan's quarters last month."

"Shore, Byrne. Glad to see yuh."

Byrne was large and stalwart of body. His deep-blue eyes were youthful and eager, and he had a strong nose and wide mouth. In his blue tunic and cavalry Stetson he made a handsome picture.

The two rode side by side for a time, but

18

bullets were coming thicker and thicker and suddenly gray-clad infantrymen burst from a thicket behind jagged rock nests, shooting at them. Byrne cried out in pain, doubling over in his sadde. The Rio Kid caught him as he was about to fall from his horse. Byrne had taken a bullet through the shoulder.

The Rio Kid's pistol rapped back at the Confederates, as he saw that a knot of Union soldiers was dashing toward them. Determined to save Adam Byrne from capture or death, the Rio Kid fired rapidly. But as the enemy became aware of the approaching forces a volley whirled at Pryor.

A slug whipped a hole in his hat; another kissed his left hand. A third ball struck his left side, and he heard the crunch of breaking ribs. Then he could no longer remember anything except that he was slumping on the dun.

Chapter II
Dangerous Mission

November had come, and General Robert E. Lee was never again to threaten the North with invasion.

For weeks it had been nip and tuck whether the Rio Kid would ever ride or even walk again. That Confederate ball he had received at the Battle of Gettysburg had torn at his vitals, but the ribs had deflected it. Having youth and terrific vitality, he had survived. And at last scarred flesh had closed over the gap in his side.

Now Bob Pryor, the Rio Kid, listened with a thrilled heart to the deep-voiced, tall man on the platform before which he stood.

"Fourscore and seven years ago our fathers brought forth on this continent a new nation conceived in liberty and dedicated to the proposition that all men are created equal. Now we are engaged in a great civil war testing whether that nation, or any nation so conceived and so dedicated, can long endure. We are met on a great battlefield of that war. We have come to dedicate a portion of that field as a final resting-place for those who here gave their lives that that nation might live. . . ."

Abraham Lincoln, sixteenth President of the United States, had come to speak at the former battlefield of Gettysburg, where the Union had won its greatest and most necessary victory only the last July.

The compelling, hypnotizing voice rolled on:

"It is altogether fitting and proper that we should do this. But, in a larger sense, we cannot dedicate, we cannot consecrate, we cannot hallow this ground. The brave men, living and dead, who struggled here have consecrated it far above our poor power to add or detract. The world will little note nor long remember what we say here, but it can never forget what they did here. . . ."

"He's a great man, Adam," murmured the Kid to his companion.

Lieutenant Adam Byrne, whom he had helped on the battlefield, nodded. Young Byrne would never be an Army man again, for his wound had made one shoulder and arm too stiff for Army requirements. The socket ball had been clipped.

When Byrne had received an honorable

discharge from service, he had stayed near his friend, Bob Pryor, faithfully tending him while he hovered between life and death. Even now the surgeons said it would be more months before the Rio Kid could rejoin his regiment, but he was regaining his power rapidly and could ride again.

The large crowd seemed apathetic to President Lincoln's words. The tall figure, bony and elongated, was clad in somber black. His sunken-cheeked face was bearded, and his eyes steady as he spoke. But at that time, the public wanted orations to be flowery, bombastic, endless. Lincoln's simple, direct appeal did not stir his listeners.

". . . It is for us the living rather to be dedicated here to the unfinished work which they who fought here have thus far so nobly advanced. It is rather for us to be here dedicated to the great task remaining before us — that from these honored dead we take increased devotion to that cause for which they gave the last full measure of devotion — that we here highly resolve that these dead shall not have died in vain, that this Nation under God shall have a new birth of freedom, and that government of the people, by the people, for the people, shall not perish from the earth."

President Lincoln bowed and returned to his chair. A low murmur of disappointment rustled through the crowd. Those listeners loved "highfalutin" words, bombast, the banging of fists on railings. With amazement the Rio Kid realized that few comprehended how great Lincoln's speech had been, that apparently many considered it decidedly second-rate.

A speaker who was in public favor came next. With his chest blown out like a pouter pigeon's, he was greeted with tremendous applause as he began shouting, raving and ranting.

Pryor turned to young Adam Byrne.

"Let's stroll over to the canteen and wet our whistles," he suggested. "That fellow hurts my ears."

Near sundown, still with Byrne, Bob Pryor was sought out by an aide who told him that General Custer wished to speak to him. The General was one of many distinguished political and military men who had come to hear the President dedicate the battlefield as a national shrine.

Custer, *beau sabreur* of the Army, handsome as a blond god with his light hair and sweeping mustache, and wearing dress uniform, shook hands with him. The Rio Kid's heart swelled at sight of his commander again.

"I'll be glad to be back in the Army, sir," he said.

"It may be some time before you are," replied Custer. "How do you feel, Pryor? Are you getting your strength back? Can you ride?"

"Oh, yes, sir. I'm really fine. Mebbe the sawbones'll let me rejoin the regiment, General."

Custer shook his head. "Come with me. There may be a more important work for you now than fighting, Captain."

Custer led the Rio Kid to a large tent around which numbers of people had congregated. Orderlies stood on guard at the closed flaps.

Inside, the Rio Kid stood at attention, blinking in the yellow light cast by a charcoal brazier that had been lighted to heat the tent, for it was growing murky, and a raw wind was springing up. Around the brazier sat high-ranking generals, politicians in civilian clothes — and Abraham Lincoln.

With deep reverence the Rio Kid saluted his Commander-in-Chief. A Scotch plaid shawl was drawn about Lincoln's bony shoulders, clad in the rusty black suit. On his head was a black stovepipe hat. His gaunt, bearded face was sharply accentuated in the shadowy enclosure as he shook hands with Bob Pryor.

"Sit down, General Custer — and you Captain Pryor," he said in his deep, gentle voice. His calm eyes studied the Rio Kid.

"Captain Pryor is one of our bravest and most efficient scouts, Mr. President," General Custer said. "He was wounded at Gettysburg and it will be at least two more months before he can rejoin his command. However, he believes he is strong enough to undertake any mission you may have in mind."

"Yes, sir, I'd be glad of such a chance," Pryor eagerly agreed.

A bluff man in civilian clothing stepped forward, as though to speak, but Lincoln waved him back.

"I'll tell Captain Pryor what I want," the President said. "Captain, I am sending trusted men to various gold and silver-producing regions to check on bullion. The United States must have every ounce available to carry on the War and to bolster the currency. The Comstock Lode is most valuable to us. Now a big strike has been made in Montana, in a place known as Alder Gulch. It is not far from Bannack. The country is wild, undeveloped, with no proper authorities at hand, no law save inefficient local officers. Information has reached us that the millions in gold from Alder Gulch are being diverted to the enemy's mints. This bullion must be turned back into the proper channels."

"Yuh wish me to go to Montana, then?" Pryor asked.

"Yes, Captain, if you feel up to it. However, the region is snowbound through the winter, and it will be spring before you can hope to reach Alder Gulch."

"I'll be there, waitin', Mr. President," the Rio Kid promised promptly. "I'll carry it through if it finishes me."

Lincoln looked earnestly at the eager young man.

"I know you will," he murmured, and held out his hand. "You will report to me in Washington when you return. I'm counting on you, Captain Pryor."

"Yes, sir."

Bob Pryor saluted smartly. He was deeply affected by Lincoln's trust in him.

The President smiled, shook hands again, and the Rio Kid left the tent. . . .

The Rio Kid pulled up the sweated, lanky dun, Saber, his warhorse, to study a sign he had come upon on the rocky trail. He was in the mountains, approaching, at long last, his destination. The run from the East had been interminable, and he had lost irritating weeks waiting for the snow-blocked trails of the Rockies to let him through to Alder Gulch.

Under his leg rode the short-barreled Army carbine which had supplied him and his trail-mate with meat throughout most of the journey. For young Lieutenant Adam Byrne, heart-broken since he could no longer serve in his country's Army, because of the wounds he had received, had come with Pryor. The Rio Kid had been glad to have Byrne along, though he had kept secret his real mission out here — the private mission entrusted to him by President Lincoln. And Byrne had been anxious to come, for like so many ex-soldiers of adventurous spirit, he wanted to try his hand at gold-mining.

The spring was at hand, but snow still covered the land, and was piled deep in the mountain canyons. In the western part of what later was to be the State of Montana, was the tremendous Bitter Root Range, part of the great Rockies, and their peaks, mantled with snow, towered ten thousand feet into the air.

Below timberline, evergreen flourished, shadowing narrow gulches that were as black as ink. The air was cold, bracingly sweet. Grizzly bear, cougar, mountain sheep and other big game abounded, while beaver, muskrat and smaller animals teemed in the streams and the forests.

In the Tobacco Roots, a smaller subsidiary range, was Alder Gulch. The Rio Kid had learned that there, one day, gold had been discovered by a man named William Fairweather and some companions who had been hunting for "tobacco money" with their washing-pans.

The deep, constricted valley was about ten miles long, winding and wicked as a snake. Towns touched one another through Alder Gulch — Virginia City, Adobetown, Summit, and others were strung along Alder Creek, which emptied into the Stinking Water.

It was Crow and Sioux hunting grounds, with the Blackfeet tribe on the north.

In the distance, when they had been crossing the higher trails, the Rio Kid and Adam Byrne had seen the plumes of smoke from cabins and wickiups perched on the hills over the claims. Some twelve thousand people inhabited Alder Gulch proper, every man jack of them thinking only of the yellow lure which had brought him so far from home into a savage beetling land.

Adam Byrne, his unshaven chin sunk wearily on his breast, came around the turn and pulled up beside his friend.

Byrne was worn out. He held his left shoulder oddly, for his wound bothered him in the damp cold. But youth had brought him through, as it had brought Captain Bob Pryor.

"We're almost there," observed the Rio Kid cheerily, and pointed to the sign beside the trail, over which he had been puzzling. At last he had made it out to read:

TU GRASS HOP PER DIGINS
30 MYLE
KEPE THE TRALE NEX THE BLUFF

The raw wind blew in their reddened faces. Softly Bob Pryor whistled an Army tune which Saber loved. The dun would come running when he heard that tune, or sometimes heard the Rio Kid sing the words:

Said the big black charger to the little white mare,
The sergeant claims your feed bill really ain't fair.

They started on, and before the next swing in the road, Saber — his ribs were

29

visible through his mousy hide now —
sniffed, and rippled the black stripe down
his spine.

"Somebody's comin'," Pryor warned
Adam Byrne, catching the dun's signal.

CHAPTER III
THE INNOCENTS

The trail was wide enough for a stage, but rutted and banked with old snow. Coming around a bluff, the Rio Kid looked down a long slope into the valley and observed a pack-train plodding up the incline. A dozen men on horseback were escorting "Rocky Mountain canaries," as the burros were facetiously called, because of their irritating braying. And they were likely to burst into that kind of "song" at any moment.

The donkeys clopped on, the burlap-bound packs on their backs oscillating with the motion. Then suddenly, between the Rio Kid and Byrne, and the approaching train, men carrying short-barreled rifles and strapped pistols swarmed from the great rocks lining the road. There were thirty-five to forty of them, the startled Rio Kid estimated. And they might almost have materialized out of thin air.

As he pulled up, staring at the bearded

31

faces, which had a sameness to them that was amazing, the men drew kerchiefs up as masks, hiding the lower jaws to the noses. The rough clothing, dirty boots and Stetsons the men wore gave them all a similarity, but the Rio Kid picked out two or three who stood out from the rest. The reddened eyes of one of them, who seemed to be a leader, burned with a horrible light.

The ambushers were not seen by the men who were coming uphill. They disposed themselves in strategic positions about the road, their guns rising.

"A hold-up, shore as guns!" shot out the Rio Kid.

The rider leading the train was on the point of making the turn right into the ambush when Bob Pryor threw his carbine to shoulder and sent a bullet down among the masked bandits. One yipped as he took the lead in a shoulder, rolling over until a boulder stopped him.

The explosion from above had an electrifying effect. The pack-train stopped short and the dozen horsemen accompanying it quickly drew their weapons. The Rio Kid's shot had warned them to be ready for trouble. Shouting with fury, the angry outlaws sprang up and opened fire. One of the miners with the donkeys threw up both hands, and crashed dead from his horse. Another, hit in the leg, fought his startled, shaggy horse, which also had felt the burning slug.

Spurring on, with Adam Byrne close behind him, the Rio Kid fired again and again. His accurately placed bullets, sent from his higher position, raised havoc among the masked killers.

"Take to the rocks, gents!" Pryor bellowed to the miners.

His stentorian voice carried over the roar of battle commandingly. The startled men in the pack-train left their horses, ducking for shelter from the guns of the attacking gang.

The masked men were swinging on the Rio Kid and Byrne, shooting back at them. Shrieking pellets whined close about their ears.

"Reminds you of Gettysburg," Byrne growled, his guns roaring steadily.

"We better take cover ourselves," Bob Pryor said quickly.

Hastily dismounting and leaving their horses behind a big rock, they scuttled to cover themselves, where they rained slugs into the masked killers. The pack-train men were shooting now, smashing bullets up at the foe. Lead and rock fragments were as thick as hail.

A harsh curse came from the bandit leader, whose fiery dark eyes the Rio Kid could glimpse over a bandanna mask. At the leader's order, but still shooting hotly, the whole gang fled down the brush-covered, stony slope toward the creek, disappearing in the gulch.

The dead miner lay sprawled on the side of the road. The pack-train men who had taken bullets were swearing and grunting as they sought to stanch the blood. But from the shouts the Rio Kid could hear as he ran back after Saber, he knew that those miners were fully conscious that whoever had been firing from above had saved them from the deadly ambush.

The pack-train men watched curiously as Pryor and Byrne approached, reaching four outlaws who lay dead in the rocks. Several other masked men had taken lead away with them.

Pryor stopped and dismounted, to have a look at the dead ambushers. Pulling off the masks he saw that though all of them wore beards, as he had noted at first sight of them before they had pulled up their bandannas, it was plain why these rough, hard fellows had looked so much alike. Mustaches and chin whiskers were of different hues, but had been cut in exactly the same fashion, as though from a set pattern. The Rio Kid's quick eye also noted the special sailor's flat knot in which the kerchiefs were fastened.

"Huh!" he remarked. "Looks like they *wanted* to look just alike. Shaved the same, the same bandanna knot, and —"

"How do you do, suh!" a gruff voice said behind him.

The Rio Kid turned. The pack-train leader had walked up to where he was examining the dead bandits.

"Howdy," Pryor said, with his quick smile, but he was as quickly thinking. "Now where have I seen *you* before?"

The man was perhaps fifty, with a short-clipped goatee, a bristly graying mustache, and a bonzed, well-shaped forehead. He had a curved, heavy nose, brown eyes, prominent ears and the hair under his battered brown hat was cut short.

He wore a miner's jacket buttoned to the throat, muddy boots and corduroy pants.

As he took a second keen look at the Rio Kid, his bearded chin dropped and he blinked unbelievingly. Then he thrust out his hand and pumped the surprised Pryor's arm.

"You!" he exclaimed. "It *is* you! I'd never forget you, suh!"

"Yuh got the better of me, mister," remarked Pryor, with a dry grin.

"Don't you remember — at Gettysburg? I'm General David Roberts, C.S.A. — or was, till I was wounded."

He turned then, and the Rio Kid saw that the lower part of the coat sleeve for his left arm was empty save for a steel hook sticking out.

"My arm was amputated at the elbow, suh," he explained. "The breast wound that looter gave me healed, but the smashed bone did not."

"Well, dang my hide, General!" Pryor exclaimed wholeheartedly. "I'm shore glad to see yuh alive and kickin'." He nodded toward his companion. "This is Adam Byrne. He fought on the Union side but he's in the same fix as you — he's invalided out."

He had had only a swift look at General Roberts on the field that day he had saved the Confederate officer from a looter, and now change in garb had kept him from recognizing the man at once.

Roberts gravely shook hands with Adam Byrne.

"It's a small world, ain't it?" marveled the Rio Kid.

"I reckon so," Roberts said. He couldn't

take his eyes off the Rio Kid. "Looks like a right good part of the world have come here after gold, too."

Pryor was wearing an Army Stetson and blue pants with the cavalry stripe down them, tucked into Army boots, but since he wore a pea-jacket over his blue shirt, he was not in uniform. It was a common sight to see ex-soldiers wearing parts or even all of their former official clothing.

"We came out here last autumn — some fifty or sixty of us — got in before the passes were blocked," Roberts explained. "We've settled at the west end of Alder Gulch. The War seems a long way off here, Captain. A terrible and a sad thing — one we must try to forget, if we can."

The miners who had been with the train had crowded around now, listening to what was being said. For the most part they were younger men than Roberts, although several were around thirty-five.

"Any idea who them hombres are who tried to hit yuh?" inquired Pryor. His Texas drawl seemed a little odd here, just as it had in the Army. But it was characteristic of him — and attractive.

"I've got a darned good idea," Roberts said decidedly. "They —"

"Good afternoon, friends!" said a low,

gentlemanly voice.

Startled, every man quickly turned, to see a horseman who had just come down the trail. He dismounted, dropping his reins, and joined them. He was perhaps thirty-five, just below six feet, slender, and his plump face had regular features. His blue eyes were mild, and the sunlight caught a red glint in his brownish hair. He sported a neat red-brown mustache. His dark suit, well brushed, the polished riding boots and straight-set clean hat, gave him a genteel, pleasing aspect.

On his lapel was pinned a star that read: SHERIFF.

"I heard some shots," he said in his cool, low voice. "Have you gentlemen had any trouble?"

"A gang of high-graders ambushed us, Sheriff," replied Roberts, "but Captain Pryor here and his friend routed them before they hit. . . . Pryor, this is Sheriff Henry Plummer, the law in these parts. He's sheriff of Virginia City and Bannack, too. Alder Gulch is in his bailiwick."

Henry Plummer's dark eyes turned upon the Rio Kid.

"Good work, sir," he congratulated. "There's been some trouble around here, but that's natural, of course, where gold is being mined by the millions. However I'm in favor of the law being observed."

"Certainly," agreed General Roberts vigorously. "On the other hand, Sheriff, if these outlaws get much thicker and bolder, the citizens may decide to take matters into their own hands."

Henry Plummer looked shocked.

"Mobs?" he cried. "Why, sir, mobs are worse than the criminals they go after. No law-abiding citizen would think of joining one! It's anarchy!" He cooled down at once. "But what was all the fuss about here?"

"We were on our way out with fifteen thousand in gold-dust and nuggets," explained Roberts, "when a gang of the Innocents, who were lying in wait for us, attacked."

"The Innocents?" repeated the Rio Kid, intrigued by the title.

Roberts hesitated, as though he felt he might have said too much. Then he explained soberly:

"That's what a band of ambushing outlaws, who are raiding hereabouts, call themselves, Captain. I made it my business to get a fellow I was sure was a member of the gang to drinkin' one evenin'. He talked a bit. I knew those dead men that fell to your guns, Captain."

He glanced at the sheriff and explained, as though the lawman would understand.

"They were close cronies of Boone Helm."

"Sheriff," Pryor said, "I reckon I could identify the leader of the gang that attacked this pack-train. His eyes would give him away to me. They burn like so much fire."

"Boone Helm!" broke in Roberts, with a sharp curse. "He was with them! There you are, Plummer. We've given you a start."

"Splendid!" said Plummer. "And don't you fail to keep in touch with me, Pryor. You'll find me in my office at Virginia City or in Bannack."

"They call me the Rio Kid, Sheriff," Bob Pryor said. "I'm from Texas, originally."

"All right, Rio Kid." The lawman smiled. "I'll see you again." He swung to General Roberts, asking softly, "Do you plan to go on, Roberts, since the robbers have been beaten off?"

As Roberts hesitated, the Rio Kid said to him:

"It's a long pull to Salt Lake City, General, where yore bullion would be safe. If I was you I'd go back and wait till I could dig up a bigger guard."

"You're right," agreed Roberts. "Two of our men are wounded, and we must bury poor Jerry. We'll return to camp and make another start in a week or two."

"Let me know when you're ready," said Sheriff Plummer, "and I'll see you have an escort, General."

The pack-train was turned around and started right back into Alder Gulch. Behind, towered the Bitter Roots, the escarpment between what were later to be the States of Idaho and Montana, in the very heart of the Rocky Mountains.

Chapter IV
Alder Gulch

It was almost dark when the cavalcade returning to Alder Gulch, turned off onto a narrow path. Sheriff Plummer took his leave of them there, riding on toward Virginia.

Soon they came to the little camp presided over by David Roberts, formerly of the Confederate Army. Wickiups and rough cabins were bunched close together on a wooded hill over the stream. Smoke issued from stone chimneys.

When the Rio Kid and Adam Byrne had cared for their horses, they were glad to get inside out of the biting wind. Roberts invited them in with an elegant courtesy that was expressive of Southern hospitality.

The former general's quarters consisted of a long, large room with a wood-burning fireplace, where the chief cooking was done. At one end was a small lean-to chamber, a bedroom for the girl who came to greet them.

"My daughter, Dorothy," Roberts said gravely.

She kissed her father, standing on tiptoe to reach his lips, and smiled at the two stalwart young men. She was a pretty girl with big, long-lashed brown eyes, red lips, and dark hair that was trimly pinned on her head. She wore a dark-blue wool dress with small hoops in the skirt, and blue slippers.

"Are you all right, Father? The men say there was some trouble." Her sweet voice held a Southern accent.

"I'm fine. But poor Jerry was shot by bandits, and two others were wounded. We turned back on the advice of this gentleman." Roberts indicated the Rio Kid. "This is Captain Pryor, Dorothy, and it's like a miracle he's come here. It's the second time he has saved my life. You remember the Yankee officer I told you about — the one who prevented that looter from cuttin' my throat? This is he!"

Gravely she took the Rio Kid's hand, murmuring her gratitude.

"I'll never forget, suh," she told him.

Adam Byrne stood by the door, hat in hand. He was staring at the pretty girl, and the Rio Kid's swift perceptions told him that Byrne had been instantly smitten.

"This is my trail-mate, Lieutenant Adam

43

Byrne, ma'am," Pryor said, with his quick smile. "He was wounded out of the War like yore father was."

Dorothy Roberts turned to the stalwart, handsome Byrne, and gave him her hand. She thanked him for the part he had played that afternoon in routing the outlaws.

"I'll have supper ready in a jiffy," she said then, and at once busied herself with the evening meal.

While the Rio Kid and Adam Byrne waited, they learned more from their host of how he and his daughter had come to be in this wilderness.

David Roberts, who came from the State of Virginia, had been a planter until the Civil War started. Having had previous military experience during the Mexican War, he had been given a regiment and, quickly proving his ability, had been breveted a brigadier.

He had known that Gettysburg had been the last chance the South had of winning, for the Blockade, the ever increasing armies massed by the more populated North, had been pressing relentlessly in. Throughout the Confederacy food, clothing, all vital goods were used up and no more could be obtained.

Unable to further help the cause he had

espoused after loss of his arm, Roberts had packed up and taken his people West. The fewer mouths to feed in the South, he had reasoned, the better.

His wife had died during the first year of the War. Dorothy was his only child, but with him now was a nephew, Taze Roberts. Because of a chipped kneecap, the younger Roberts had been honorably discharged. Several more distant relatives of the Roberts family also were digging gold in Alder Gulch.

During the evening, sitting by a blazing wood fire, the Rio Kid and Adam Byrne met more of the small community. There were about fifty in the settlement which had been named Jefferson by General Roberts. A dozen were women, wives who had accompanied their husbands, or daughters of older men.

And several children were among them.

They gathered in the Roberts' main room to hear the news from the visitors. The Rio Kid learned that a man of around forty, Zeb Warren, stocky and with a baldish head and wrinkles around his gray eyes, was second in command to Roberts. His wife and three children were with him, in the cabin he had built.

Pryor shook hands with a man named

Lee, one named Standish, a couple of Jacksons. They were good folks, hard-working and filled with new hope, hope of making a big strike in Alder Gulch to recoup their lost fortunes.

The War was taboo. They did not speak of it if they could help it, although the story of how Pryor had saved General Roberts from death was recounted.

The Rio Kid especially liked Taze Roberts, a smiling easy-going young man about Pryor's own age and size. His wife, Elizabeth, a slender, dark-eyed girl, had come with him to the dangerous wilderness.

"My clothes are shore a mess," remarked the Rio Kid after awhile, when the talk of the day's adventure had died down.

"Why not let the women clean 'em up for you?" asked Taze. "Betsy'll be glad to throw 'em in with my wash."

"Of course," Elizabeth said at once.

Pryor grinned. "But I got no spare duds," he demurred. "And I reckon I'll be ridin' on in the mornin'."

"I'll loan yuh some," offered Taze. "We're the same size."

This was what the Rio Kid was angling for, so in the morning he donned butternut breeches, a gray wool shirt and Taze's heavy gray Army coat.

"I'll be back in a few days, Taze," he said. "Then I'll change back my clothes for yores. Say, for a joke, how about we switch hats? Yuh got a Confederate Stetson hangin' in yore kitchen."

This appealed to Taze's sense of humor, and the Rio Kid prepared to depart.

Adam Byrne was still lying in his blankets. When Pryor went to rouse him, Byrne's eyes looked up with a bright glint in them, and the red spots on his cheekbones told the Rio Kid his trail-mate had fever.

"Yuh better not ride today, Adam," he advised. "Yuh feel bad?"

"Yeah. Weak as a pup, Bob."

The Rio Kid reported this to Roberts.

"We'll bring him inside the cabin," the general said at once. "Dorothy, you must nurse him."

The Rio Kid was just as well satisfied to go on alone. Adam Byrne was not aware that his comrade was on a dangerous military mission, one that amounted to Intelligence work. It was for this reason that Pryor had obtained the change of clothing that would make him look like an ex-Confederate. He did not like to deceive anyone, but his country came first.

For a time, he had wondered if perhaps General Roberts knew anything about the deflection of gold bullion from the Northern mints. But all the talk he had heard was of mining, strikes, nuggets of prodigious size. These people he had met had seemed open, above board, merely hunting a new start in a troubled world.

It would, he knew, be a difficult task to discover the leak. In order to do so he needed connections which, so far, were non-existent.

The sun was bright in an intensely blue sky as he rode through Alder Gulch. Smoke issued from the stacks of the cabins on the hills, while below, men were already feverishly digging out gravel, washing it in Longtoms, rockers and pans.

"Pay dirt" was in every man's mind. No man had time to think of civil affairs, of the community. Most considered themselves only temporary inhabitants, anyhow, meaning to depart for more pleasant surroundings when a strike had been made.

The Rio Kid rode the twisting, snaky road above Alder Creek, rattling in its gravelly bed. Trees and brush were thick on the banks and up the hills.

With one small settlement joining another, for ten miles, saloons, honkytonks, shebangs, stores of all sorts lined the frozen dirt way.

At one end of the Gulch stood Virginia City, where Henry Plummer had his sheriff's office. Raw-board and log buildings, some of two stories, others with raised fronts — stores, saloons, dancehalls, and dwellings — lined the town's Main Street. Signs marked the buildings that faced each other across the rutted dirt way that was lined with teams, wagons, and riding horses.

When the Rio Kid arrived in town, the morning stage was making ready to depart. Driver and shotgun messenger were in position, and several passengers were in the Concord coach. With a faint idea that he might find a clue there, the Rio Kid gravitated to the stage station.

A heavy box was being strapped into place on the stage, no doubt gold bullion going out. But the Rio Kid gave it only a passing glance, for what caught his eye at that moment were two men lounging in the sun. Their mustaches and chin whiskers were cut to the same pattern, and each had a flat sailor's knot in his kerchief. The marks of the Innocents, the Rio Kid was sure — the gang which had attacked Roberts' party!

Sheriff Henry Plummer, who had been talking to the stage-coach driver, backed away with a wave of his hand, and the driver cracked his whip. But as soon as the stage had departed, creaking off, the two men the Rio Kid had been watching hurried to their horses, leaped to saddle, and spurred off up a narrow path that would take them across the hills.

Intrigued by this byplay, the Rio Kid at once turned Saber to follow, but at a long distance. Reaching the summit of a hill, he waited behind a screen of bare alders as he watched the two flog their mustangs along the horse trail in the bush. In this way riders could cut off some miles by heading across country in winding, serpentine Alder Gulch.

The land was gorgeous, with great rocks sticking up, evergreens thick on the slopes, and the leafless brush and trees stark against the white of the melting snow. And because of that snow the Rio Kid could hang back out of sight and follow his quarry by the fresh hoofmarks they left.

The riders ahead flogged through a wide dip, up another rocky slope, and took to a frozen dirt road along a ridge, with Alder Gulch and the mining towns far below, in the distance. Finally the pair ahead on their steaming horses stopped at an isolated, lonely building, a two-storied place surrounded by tall trees. It was made of log slabs shaped by adzes, and a balcony ran

50

the length of the front. A crude sign proclaimed:

CLUB SALOON

Outside stood thirty saddled mustangs,
reins over a hitch-rack. In the rear were
stables and smaller shacks. Lurking back
out of sight, the Rio Kid watched as the
men he had followed from Virginia signaled
men inside. A couple of dozen emerged,
most of them wearing the peculiar beard
cut the Rio Kid had noted.

The gang mounted and headed off
through the hills. A shock went through the
Rio Kid.

"Are they goin' to hit that stage?" he muttered.

CHAPTER V
EYES OF DEATH

Riding fast, the twenty-five men in the party Bob Pryor watched, cut through a side gulch and hit the main road before the Rio Kid could pick up on them. He hunted for a way around them, but before he could find a route, shots banged out in the crisp air, accompanied by shouting.

Hiding Saber, for the going was too rough for a horse, he climbed to the bluff and crept to a point where he could look down on the road from Alder Gulch.

The men from the isolated building the Rio Kid had seen had already stopped the stage, and shot the driver and messenger off the box. The box of bullion had been loaded onto the back of a horse.

The passengers were being dragged out, their hands elevated. The Innocents were masked now, as they searched their victims under their guns. The robbers were bullying a couple of men, slapping them around for the sport of it. One retaliated, and was instantly knocked down and kicked in the face. A high-grader swung and shot him through the head.

This was the signal for a scene more horrible than any Indian massacre, since it was cold-blooded, and done for the fun of it. The Rio Kid was too far off for a pistol to reach, and all he could do was watch, with gritting teeth and black fury in his heart, as the Innocents poured lead into the helpless passengers.

A robber jumped to the stage, and smoke began to show as the straw ticking was fired. Leaving six dead, and the coach a blazing ruin, the wild gang dashed off at full-tilt, splitting up into sections and disappearing.

The Rio Kid worked back and picked up the dun. The killers had a long start on him, but he had seen the place they frequented — Robbers' Roost, he called it grimly. And he had to find them, for it was in his mind that once they were brought to time it would be possible to check the final destination of much Montana gold that the Federal authorities believed to be filtering into the coffers of the Confederacy, strengthening its credit abroad and making prolongation of the War possible.

These Innocents, this Wild Gang, as he

had also heard them called the night before, appeared to have a finger in every pie, from what he had seen, and from what Roberts had told him. Road-agents, high-graders, and other dishonest characters were probably in their ranks.

They should know of any smuggling of precious metals.

"I'll head back to that Roost," the Rio Kid muttered.

When he scouted the isolated saloon late that afternoon there were but three horses outside. He placed most of his money and his spare pistols in Saber's saddle-bags, leaving only what he wished to have possible enemy searchers find in his pockets — which included a specially prepared set of papers which he carried for any such emergency as that he now probably would face.

Then he rode up and dismounted, placing Saber carefully so that he was within easy jump of a back door. With an unsteady walk, the Rio Kid, deliberately placing his life in jeopardy in order to carry out his dangerous mission for his President, opened the door and staggered into the saloon.

"Shut that door, you fool!" a gruff voice called.

A thin man with a bald head, a hooked beak and a twisted mouth drawn up from a knife scar in his left cheek, and wearing a dirty white apron, was watching him from behind a crude bar made of long pine slabs. A Navy .44 revolver rested close to hand.

A big wood fire was blazing on the stone hearth, while a couple of flickering candles lighted the whiskey bottles on the bar. At a slab table to one side sat three customers. One wore a patterned beard and a road-agent's knot in his kerchief. Another, a stout, nondescript fellow, appeared to be in a stupor.

The third was a lean man with high cheek-bones and deep-set black eyes that shone like shoebuttons. Curly black hair covered the nape of his thin neck and prominent ears stuck out at right angles to his head. His strong mouth beneath his crisp black mustache, turned down at the corners with a set look. His clothing was that of a professional gambler — black coat, ruffled white shirt and stock.

The last did not miss a single detail of the Rio Kid's carefully prepared nondescript appearance — the garments of a Confederate soldier, dirty and wet, the chin stubble, the bloodshot eyes. Pryor slapped a fist on the bar and threw down some bills.

"Whiskey," he growled at the bartender.

The bald-headed man eyed the money

disdainfully.

"Why, that stuff's no good here, Johnny Reb. Confederate money ain't legal tender."

"When the War's won," snarled the Rio Kid, "yuh'll take it and be glad to get it!"

The barkeeper shrugged. The Rio Kid tossed in a small sack containing gold dust, and the saloon owner weighed out three dollars on a scale, in exchange for which Pryor was served raw, gullet-singeing whiskey.

Pryor consumed it slowly, pretending to have been drinking heavily. He knew that he was playing with death.

After dark, hoofs sounded outside, then fifteen men came crowding in. The Rio Kid recognized them instantly — some of the bunch who had robbed the stage that morning, men with the beards and sailors' knots of the Innocents. They wore thick jackets and heavy boots against the cold mountain wind.

One was the tall, burning-eyed devil Pryor had seen when General Roberts' pack-train had been ambushed. The fellow wore two .44 Navy pistols and a long knife. He recalled the name, "Boone Helm," when they lined up along the short bar, and one of them said, "Lemme buy for yuh tonight, Boone."

There was a good reason for this Boone Helm to hide behind a mask, Bob Pryor thought. His face was fishy and pockmarked where the shaped beard didn't hide it. His mouth was cruel, sneering, and in the dark eyes was a mad, murderous glow. Those red-rimmed, penetrating eyes fixed the Rio Kid, slouched over the bar.

Jerking a thumb toward the apparently sodden figure, in the remnants of a Confederate uniform, Helm asked:

"Who's the barfly, Skinner?"

"Oh, some bummer who just wandered in late this afternoon," Skinner the saloon-keeper replied. "Looks like a deserter to me."

The Rio Kid was keenly alert. He was fully aware that there was a chance the men would recognize him, despite the dirt he had smeared over his face to disguise his features. But in the dim light, with the fire the chief illumination, none appeared to connect him with the hard-fighting horseman who had scattered them the previous day. He had been in the rocks, a good distance off, and in the excitement of battle, they could not more than have glimpsed him.

A couple of the Innocents, wanting a place at the bar, shoved the Rio Kid. He staggered, pretending to be stupid from drink, and they laughed raucously. Another pushed him, still another caught him by the arm, whirling him around and down the line. When he hit the wall and slid to the puncheon floor, his head bumping the mud-chinked wall, the saloon rang with merriment.

He sat there with his eyes half-closed.

"See what he's got on him, Ned," Helm growled.

A big outlaw strolled over and quickly searched the Rio Kid, taking his few dollars in dust, his single pistol, and two letters bearing a Richmond, Virginia, postmark.

"Name's Steeves, I reckon," said the outlaw called Ned coolly. "And he's a Reb."

The bony-faced man with the grim mouth got up and called:

"Oh, Helm! I've been waitin' all afternoon for yuh."

Boone Helm scowled at him, but replied, "All right, Carter. Be with yuh in a jiffy." He jerked a thumb at the Rio Kid. "Throw him out, boys."

"Wait," said Carter. "He'll freeze to death tonight. Put him in the back somewhere."

Helm spouted profanity, but made no objection when Skinner and a couple of other men dragged the seemingly helpless

Pryor into the darkness of a back lean-to and left him there. The partitions were thin, and the wood, drying in the heat of the fire, had shrunk so that big cracks let light through from the saloon.

Carter and Boone Helm came to a corner near the lean-to to speak together in low tones. The Rio Kid crawled inch by inch until he could hear what they were saying. Ear to a crack, he was able to filter out their words from the raucous talk of the main gang at the bar.

"— Very important," Carter was saying earnestly. "Must have gold. If we get enuff, France or even England may back us."

"Throwin' good money after bad," grumbled Helm.

"Yuh got over half a million in Richmond now, Helm," protested Carter. "Yuh want to save it. We got the other shipments through."

"Yeah, but they've tightened up, George."

"I've got it all arranged," insisted Carter. "A ship will be waitin' for us at San Francisco the day we get in with the bullion. We sail to the Isthmus, pack across, and transfer to a blockade-runner up the Gulf. We have agents at the Comstock and in California, and —"

"Why should I send gold to Richmond? I

can spend it here."

"Yuh know well yuh can't last here. Yuh'll hafta pull out in another year or two, when they organize real law. Yuh want a safe bunk, don't yuh? The Confederacy'll win, I tell yuh. All we need's the gold. Yuh're a sympathizer, and yuh got too big a stake in winnin' to back down now."

"Quit botherin' me," snapped Helm. "I got important work to do, Carter. The Chief sent word this mornin' that a passel of skunks reckernized me and can identify some of us on account of a little set-to we had in the hills yestiday afternoon."

The Rio Kid started. Helm was talking about General Roberts and his pack-train.

And that meant danger to the little community of Jefferson, set off by itself at the far end of Alder Gulch. Somehow Roberts would have to be warned!

CHAPTER VI
NIGHT ATTACK

Desperately trying to figure out what he could do, the Rio Kid listened keenly to every word that was said.

"Wait," he heard Carter order, as Helm's box seat scraped on the floor. "I ain't told yuh it all, Boone. Yuh must listen. Yuh stand to be rich as Croesus if the South wins. What yuh've done so far has been elegant. But what we can pull off next week will startle the world!"

"What yuh mean?" the Rio Kid heard Boone Helm growl.

"What would yuh say if we could pick up a million in gold at one scoop?"

"I'd say yuh're loco, George Carter, if yuh think there's that much gold in one spot around here."

George Carter laughed.

"Well, there is! Three or four big mines have held most of their bullion, hidden and guarded, for months. They've struck it richer'n they let on, and they mean to move it all out for the Government mint next Saturday night. They start after dark, and there'll be forty armed guards with it. They leave from Virginia City. Sanders, Williams and Biedler are responsible for it."

Boone Helm cursed roundly. "Now I believe yuh, Carter," he raged. "No wonder the boxes we took lately have been so light! They pulled the wool over our eyes, the Chief's included. As for Williams and Sanders and that Biedler skunk, we been gunnin' for 'em a long while, the lobos! They've tried to get up vigilantes to ride agin us, and Sanders is always talkin' about seein' us hung. They'll rot in the mountains for that!"

"Now will yuh work with me?" demanded the Confederate agent.

"Yeah! If only to get square with them rattlers!"

"Give me yore word of honor yuh'll turn over the bulk of the bullion to us, after payin' yore men a fair sum?" Carter pursued. "I'll make up the rest in Confederate government bonds and currency. At the end of the War yuh'll be a king, Helm."

"I promise," said Helm quickly. "My word on it, George. Work out the details and lemme know. I'll have sixty men or more

62

for the job. I'll be glad to put it over on Sanders and Williams, curse 'em!"

"Good. Shake on it, then. I know I can trust yuh. Yuh're with us."

"Shore, I'm for the South," Helm declared. "But now we got to ride, Carter. We can't leave informers live."

"Meet me here Thursday night at nine o'clock, then."

"Right. S'long."

The Rio Kid heaved a deep sigh of relief. He knew who he was after now. This George Carter was the man who had been detailed to turn as much smuggled gold to the Confederacy's coffers as possible.

Evidently the men Carter had mentioned — Sanders, Williams, and Biedler — had sought to fool the Innocents by hiding gold for three mining syndicates, and planned on taking it out secretly.

"But now," he thought, "I got to tip off Roberts."

"Aw right, boys," he heard Boone Helm call. "We're ridin'."

The fifteen with Helm hurried outside, mounted and rode away in the night so swiftly that the Rio Kid feared he might be too late to save his friends. With all possible speed he crept outside, silent so that the saloonkeeper would not hear him.

Would the killers head straight for the town of Jefferson? If so, they would arrive well ahead of him. He pushed Saber on, seeking the road into the Gulch. Then a red glow showed over the narrow, winding ravine and he knew it came from the lights of the honky-tonks and saloons lining the Gulch. He found a beaten horse path and rode swiftly to the steep slope.

He could hear the distant cries of celebrating men, with a shot now and then as someone pulled a trigger in fun.

In an hour he was in Alder Gulch, riding up the main road past the succession of saloons and dancehalls. The road was crowded, with men in miner's rough garb, with black-frocked gamblers, with riffraff. Horses and teams stood about. Music banged from every place, and booted fellows whirled around with gaily clad girls, at a dollar a dance. The Rio Kid knew such places, knew how, at the end of every dance, the master-of-ceremonies would shout, "Ladies and gents to the bar!" which was a signal to buy drinks.

Men paid chiefly in gold dust, weighed out on scales from their sacks. Some had currency, but metal was preferred. It was all mad babel and confusion. Southern sympathizers were here, and men from the North, many of them soldiers who had been wounded or invalided out of the combat. Others had come to escape conscription, or had wandered over from California and Utah.

The Rio Kid gave it all only a fleeting glance as he pushed the dun on toward Jefferson. Out of Alder Gulch, he started up the wind-blown, deserted slope. It was late, and the settlement was dark, and with relief he heard no shots to tell him that the killers had made their attack. When the attack did come, though, it would be one to the death, for from what he had seen of Boone Helm and his gang, he did not expect mercy to be shown to the Roberts family and their friends. They had become too dangerous to the Innocents to be allowed to live.

As the Rio Kid slowed and swung the dun toward Roberts' cabin home, a cursing shout from the hill told him the Innocents had arrived. Against the whiteness of the snowy ridge, he glimpsed riders pressing in, for there was a slice of moon up and the stars were out.

More than Helm's fifteen men were with the Innocents' leader now. Two or three times that many, the Rio Kid estimated.

"Picked up more men!" he decided grimly. "That's how I come to beat 'em here."

The next moment his stentorian voice was roaring through the darkness.

"Bandits! Robbers! Everybody up and at 'em!"

Seeing him, the riders in the van yelled. Their bullets hunted him, shrieking close about his moving form. He heard a couple of slugs rap into the logs of Roberts' home. Masked horsemen whose faces were blobs of darkness were filtering into the settlement.

The Rio Kid left the dun in a flying jump. As he slapped his mount on the rump Saber went dashing off out of danger.

"Roberts — Taze — Byrne!" called Pryor, as he hit the door. "Wake up, Jefferson! To yore guns! The Innocents 're here!"

The masked men swung in, seeking to kill the man who had dared bring warning. The door was unbolted and the Rio Kid dashed inside, shooting back at the bunched riders. One threw up his hands and slumped dead in his leather. Another yipped with anguish as a bullet struck his shoulder.

Firearms roared from both sides as the Rio Kid slammed the oaken door and dropped the bar-bolt. He had the two pistols he had left with Saber when he had entered Robbers Roost. Bullets futilely hit the door and thick logs as he stumbled over the puncheon floor.

"What's up, Captain Pryor?" Roberts hailed anxiously from the darkness.

"Boone Helm and a bunch of his killers are here to slaughter yuh, 'cause yuh said yuh could identify 'em!" the Rio Kid reported. "Up and at 'em."

His warning had come just in the nick of time. The furious Innocents split up into groups, seeking to storm the various shacks, but Roberts was calling orders from his window and the men of Jefferson sprang to their guns. Roberts voice was still echoing when they were shooting from narrow loophole windows at the horsemen who were plain targets against the snow.

The Rio Kid, with one hand bleeding from a skin wound, took a window side and began his accurate work upon the riders outside. They were howling and swearing, and pouring bullets in.

Someone went to the fireplace and blew up a dull-red coal, lighting a candle from it. The little flame was at once hidden under a box so as not to betray the defenders to those outside, but it was necessary light for loading guns.

The rustle of skirts told that Dorothy Roberts was loading guns for the men.

General Roberts was making his Army

pistol take toll. He was an expert marksman, but reloading was difficult because of his lost left arm. With his iron hook bracing him against the window edge, his bearded face was grim in the faint light as he defended his home. Young Adam Byrne, much better after his rest, was also in the fight. And the three men held the fort.

"They got a door open over there, General," called the Rio Kid.

Flashes, yellow-red in the darkness, showed through the smashed panels as someone inside kept shooting.

"That's Taze's cabin," Roberts cried anxiously.

"This way, men!" roared Boone Helm's ugly voice. "In and tear 'em to pieces!"

But to the Rio Kid and General Roberts the bunching Innocents, striving to crash their way in against Taze's blazing gun were targets that could not be missed. Bullets struck full into the bodies of the killers, and their shrieks rose shrill in the night. They split, leaving that spot of death, stung by the guns of the Rio Kid and the Confederate general.

"Get in there!" bellowed Helm.

But fighting against such odds did not please his followers. They liked to have every advantage against surprised unarmed victims. They ran off around the cabin.

But at other homes more masked killers were seeking admittance that would spell death to those inside!

Chapter VII
The Lion of
the North

For minutes a hot fight raged on. Swirling, maddened killers hunted a way to take the people who were barricaded in their cabins. Hay was dragged from a shed and set afire against Zeb Warren's home. The burning hay licked up against the wooden wall, threatening to smoke the Warrens out, but the blaze proved to be a tactical error, for it lighted the whole settlement so that the bandits were in the glow, full targets for the hidden settlers' guns.

"This is pie!" gloated the Rio Kid. "We can see them, and they can't see us!"

"Perfect!" agreed General Roberts. "It would have been different, though, if you hadn't come in time to warn us."

As the burning cabin wall and hay exposed the Innocents, their eyes gleamed over the kerchiefs that were drawn up to their noses. Burly figures strove to close in, but were drawn back into the shadows by the settlers' lead.

The Rio Kid was shooting with clock-like accuracy, and with speed. Roberts and Byrne, too, were doing fine work, while Dorothy loaded guns. Shotguns bellowed, rifles snapped.

"I'd like to knock that devil Helm off his mustang," muttered the Rio Kid, as he saw the dodging leader over toward Warren's shack.

He turned his Colt muzzle for careful aim. But as he fired, Helm shifted, although he jumped in his saddle as Pryor's revolver boomed.

"Touched him, anyways," thought the Rio Kid, as Helm galloped around to the other side of the cabin, out of his sight.

"Away, boys — away!" he heard Helm bellow.

The attack had proved to be a fiasco from Boone Helm's standpoint. Warned in time, the intended victims had turned the tables on the killers. Four of the Innocents lay dead in the trampled snow, while several more carried lead away as they spurred madly up the slope and dropped out of sight behind the ridge.

As the shattering gunfire stopped, Jefferson people began calling to neighbors, inquiring who was hurt. Three had felt the murderous rage of the Innocents. And when the settlers found it was the Rio Kid who had again saved them, their gratitude knew no bounds. Bob Pryor was a Union soldier, but he knew that these Confederates would believe him, would follow him anywhere now.

He needed food and rest. Pretty Dorothy Roberts cooked him a meal, then he turned in at Roberts'.

In the morning, he shaved and spruced up, resuming his former garb, which Taze's young wife had washed and mended for him.

"Mighty sorry, but I ruint yore clothes last night, Taze," he told the general's nephew. "I'll buy yuh a fresh rig in town today."

"Fergit it," Taze replied. "Yuh kept the Innocents from murderin' us all, Bob."

He held on to Taze's old clothing, though, stowing it in a saddle-bag. He would need it when Carter, the Confederate Intelligence agent, met Boone Helm at Robbers Roost on Thursday.

The Rio Kid meant to be himself in Union blue in the open, but when he wished to spy on the Wild Bunch he would be the dirty, ragged deserter from the South.

It was a crisp sunny morning when the

reckless-eyed debonair Rio Kid said good-by to the Roberts family and their friends before starting for Virginia City. Adam Byrne who had recovered from his illness that had been brought on from exhaustion and strain was going with him.

Byrne lingered for an extra word with Dorothy Roberts who had taken such excellent care of him. The big brown eyes of the pretty Southern girl looked up at the young Northern lieutenant, and color touched her smooth, soft cheeks, as she smiled.

"I'll be back," Byrne promised, "if it's all right with you."

"Oh, yes, do come again," she told him.

The Civil War had created raw wounds in the hearts of men, and of women who were fiercely loyal. Between Byrne and Dorothy was an invisible barrier. Her father had fought on one side, Byrne on the other, and the conflict was as yet undecided. It was impossible to stifle the bitterness stirred up by such a war.

The handsome Rio Kid leaned down from his saddle to speak to General Roberts.

"Lie low, General," he warned. "Keep a guard out at night, savvy? That gang means to do yuh in, for yuh're dangerous to 'em. They won't give up this easy."

"I'll do that," promised Roberts.

The Rio Kid waved to his new friends. They were out of the combat now and were his countrymen, and as far as he was concerned they were just Americans, fine folks. And now, added to his responsibility as an agent of President Lincoln, was the burden of protecting these miners of Jefferson.

"Besides," he thought, "if I smash the Innocents it'll go a long way toward pluggin' up the leak of bullion to the South. I'll hafta take Carter, too."

With Adam Byrne again his saddlemate, the Rio Kid hit the trail down Alder Gulch. Miners were going to work, intent now only on extracting from the ground as much precious metal as possible. Little attention was paid the two young riders as they cantered along the frozen, winding road, their breath frosting in the morning air.

They passed Summit, Adobetown, and other settlements chiefly noted for their honky-tonks. In the clear light the tawdriness was depressing. In the morning-after-the-night-before the walks and street were littered with junk, broken glass, empty tin cans, discharged shells, and bits of discarded food. The saloons were quiet, and the dancehall girls resting up for the next whirl.

The chief interest in life for all in Alder

Gulch was gold. That was all men thought of, either how to get it out of the gravel and rock, or how to get it out of those who labored so hard to find it.

From casual inquiry at Jefferson the Rio Kid had found out that at Virginia City he would find the three men who had been mentioned by Carter, the Confederate agent. Sanders, Williams, and Biedler, Carter had named them. The Rio Kid had business with these men because it was vitally important that he prevent the great accrual of gold of which he had heard on his perilous visit to Robbers' Roost from falling into Carter's hands.

Virginia City, the metropolis of Alder Gulch, was the largest of the settlements. Drug stores, hardware shops, general emporiums where clothing, boots, food, ammunition and feed could be bought, were squeezed in between the many saloons and dancehalls. The slanting main street was rutted and dirty.

Behind the false-fronted buildings, with smoke issuing from their chimneys, was Tin Can Alley, with stables and barns, and piles of discarded cans and garbage.

As the Rio Kid and Byrne cantered slowly down the center of the road, Pryor's quick eyes saw a painted wooden sign:

COL. WILBUR F. SANDERS
ATT'Y AT LAW
CLAIMS AND LAND DEEDS

"S'pose you go have a drink, Byrne," he said to his young companion, who appeared deeply interested in the mining camp. "I'll meet yuh in an hour at the Bearcat there."

Byrne had spoken little during the two-hour ride. He had seemed preoccupied.

"She doesn't like the War," he said now. "It's a shame, ain't it, that we have to fight men like Roberts and Taze? When you know 'em they're the salt of the earth."

The Rio Kid smiled. He knew what was worrying Adam Byrne.

"One day the War'll be over, Adam, the Union saved, and the hatred ended," he said soberly. "Now s'pose yuh ask around about minin' claims, and I will, too."

"Why can't we go together?"

"I got a man to see," evaded Pryor.

He left Byrne, and dismounted near Sanders' law office, rapping on the closed door.

"Come in," a deep voice sang out.

Inside, near a pot-bellied iron stove, sat a tall man, with the sunlight streaming through the crude windows on his splendid head. He had a high, intelligent brow, fine, serious eyes, a strong nose. A soft mustache swept down to join his chin beard, but the whiskers did not hide the determination expressed by his straight mouth. His thick, luxuriant hair was parted on the left side, his clothing was black and he wore a round white collar and black bow tie.

Wilbur F. Sanders, known as "The Lion of the North," and brains of the Montana Vigilantes, looked up at his visitor.

"Good morning, sir," he said politely, appraising the Rio Kid with a swift glance. "What can I do for you?"

"He's got a gun in that drawer and he's on the alert," decided the Rio Kid, noticing that Sanders did not move from his seat behind the desk.

He shut the door and strode to the desk, looking straight into Sanders' eyes. He found strength, honesty and a leader's eagle glint in them.

"My name's Bob Pryor, sir. Yuh're Colonel Sanders?"

"Yes. Glad to know you, Pryor."

His appraisal seemed satisfactory, for he rose to his tall height and held out a hand to Pryor.

"They call me the Rio Kid," Bob Pryor said, as he shook Sanders' hand. "I hail from the Rio Grande, but I fought under Custer and Sheridan for the Union."

Sanders' eyes glinted. "I was in the thick of it myself, but was invalided out last year. Came to Montana for my health. Sit down, please."

When they were seated Sanders watched the Rio Kid inquiringly from across the flat-topped desk.

"Colonel," the Rio Kid said, "I want to ask you a question. Yuh have two friends named Williams and Biedler?"

Sanders nodded, his face a study. "Yes, James Williams and John X. Biedler. Why do you ask?"

"I just pulled in here a couple of days ago. At the far end of the Gulch I ran into a gang of road-agents ambushin' a gold train out of Jefferson, that new camp off by itself in the hills. We had a fight and I downed some. Last night the same bunch — they call themselves the Innocents and most of 'em have their beards cut the same way and wear a flat knot in their kerchiefs — attacked Jefferson and tried to kill all the men who might identify 'em to the law."

Sanders was excited.

"You're a smart man, Pryor!" he commended. "In forty-eight hours you've learned what it took me weeks to ferret out. You say you can identify some of the so-called Innocents?"

"I shore can. Boone Helm in particular, Colonel."

Sanders leaped to his feet.

"Wait a minute! I want Williams to hear this, Rio Kid."

He seized his hat and coat and rushed out the back way. In twenty minutes he returned with two men.

"Captain Jim Williams," he said to one of them, "meet Captain Pryor, the Rio Kid."

James Williams was a huge, burly young man with a mop of thick hair and a leonine head; a mustache and chin beard. Williams was a Pennsylvanian, a farmer, although he had fought Indians and dug for gold. His deep eyes were blue and mild, but he had a genius for appraising men, and for the work which later made him Executive Officer of the Montana Vigilantes.

Under usual conditions Williams was gentle, but when aroused his rage was that of an angered lion. His blue eyes turned black, and his voice grated harsh. Murderers quailed before him. In years to come a tablet to his memory in the capitol at Helena was to have engraved on it:

The sluice was left unguarded,
When Williams' work was done,
And trails were safe for honest men

Through victories he had won.

If Sanders was the brains and spirit of the Montana Vigilantes, James Williams was the organization's strong arm. He was as brave as a lion, and had a cold nerve that was appalling. Diffident and shy normally, in dangerous situations Williams was a hero, an ace.

John X. Biedler, the third of the triumvirate, was a stocky, older man, with a square head, flat on the top. He had thick black brows, and a cross-looking face, trimmed with drooping mustaches and short-clipped chin beard. Small patches of whiskers grew under his ears, and his nose curved over his lip.

Sanders introduced Biedler to the Rio Kid.

They shook hands, and all sat down, Sanders making sure no one was close enough to hear.

CHAPTER VIII
FLAT ACCUSATION

Quietly the Rio Kid told something of what he had discovered, although he kept his secret mission from the three men he had come to Virginia City to see. His purpose, he announced to them, was to protect Roberts and the folks of Jefferson, and also himself, from the Innocents.

"I knowed Helm was one of 'em!" exclaimed Williams, slapping his thigh with a big hand. His blue eyes glowed, turning dark with his rising anger.

"Yuh savvy an hombre named George Carter?" inquired the Rio Kid casually.

"Carter?" repeated Sanders. He looked at his friends, but the three shook their heads. "Why? Who is he? One of the gang?"

"I don't reckon so. But on the other hand, how about that million dollars in gold yuh're hidin' for the Syndicate?"

Sanders started, and a red flush mounted to his high forehead.

"Who told you of that?" he demanded.

"It's no secret. Helm knows about it."

Biedler swore, his square hand that was made to grip a shotgun and pistol tightening. Biedler was a real fighting man.

"What's wrong around here, anyway?" the Rio Kid went on. "This gang is organized to a T, gents. They keep tabs on gold shipments and rob the stages as they wish. I seen one such robbery yesterday mornin', when they shot down six men mostly for the fun of it. They wear their beards alike, and knotted bandannas, don't they — so they can tell each other? Catch a couple and they'll talk. They must be smashed."

Sanders looked sour. "You're right, Pryor, but unfortunately the citizens won't organize, won't listen. The fact is that the Innocents are powerful, and protect one another. No one dares even talk against them. Many who have reported them have been found shot or with their throats slit. We have no strong law here. Plummer does the best he can, I suppose, but the road-agents are thick as fleas. They have spies everywhere.

"We've tried to rouse the miners, but they're obsessed with gold fever and won't band together. Not even when they know that whenever a prospector makes a big strike, or a man has luck at the gaming tables, he is likely to be robbed — killed, if he objects. Shipments on the stages aren't much safer."

"Let's go talk to Plummer," Biedler growled. "With Pryor able positively to identify Helm and some of the rest of 'em, the sheriff'll hafta act. Are yuh afraid to come out in the open against 'em, Rio Kid?"

"Be glad to," Pryor promptly replied.

"I could tell that at a glance," Sanders said. "Let's go over and see Plummer now."

"Will yuh tell me where yuh've got that million in gold hid, Sanders?" the Rio Kid asked. "I'd like to keep an eye on it. Helm and his gang will be after it as shore as shootin'."

"All right, Rio Kid. If Helm knows, you might as well." Sanders took his arm and led him to a window, looking down the wide street. "See that warehouse by the creek, marked 'Thos. Green'? The bullion's in there, with bales of hay on top of it. We have guards watching it."

"Bueno."

"C'mon," Biedler said, opening the door. "Plummer just went inside his office."

Quickly the four walked to the sheriff's office, a square, wooden affair. Inside, they found Henry Plummer, Sheriff of Virginia

City and Bannack, the gentlemanly officer whom the Rio Kid had met in the mountains.

Plummer had just sat down at his table. He blinked, and rose, hands hanging loosely at his hips that were girded with Navy pistols, his star shining on his coat.

"How do you do, gentlemen," he said softly.

His mild blue eyes quickly appraised grim faces confronting him. The Rio Kid had a queer feeling in the pit of his stomach as Plummer smiled at him.

"So you're here," the sheriff said gently. "I was worried about you, Pryor, not seeing you since the holdup. Where have you been hiding yourself?"

"I was worn out," the Rio Kid replied, "and stuck around Jefferson for a while to rest up."

Plummer looked inquiringly at the other men, to hear what they had come about. Sanders began to relate some of the information detailed by the Rio Kid.

"Pryor can identify Helm positively, Plummer," Sanders said bluntly. "So can some of the Roberts' people. We have an iron-clad case against Helm, so why don't we bring him to trial?"

"He won't get off this time," growled

Biedler angrily. "There've been too many of these trials with lyin' witnesses and crooked lawyers. Now it'll be different. Sanders will prosecute and Jim and me'll make sure justice is done."

Plummer frowned, shaking his head. "I won't have any mob violence in my bailiwick, gentlemen. Robbery and murder are bad, but lynch law is anarchy. However, I'll swear in a posse and go after Helm — that is, if Pryor here is certain he can swear to him and will be on hand when the trial opens."

"I will," agreed the Rio Kid. "I can tell yuh a good deal about the Innocents, Plummer."

"Can you?" said the sheriff.

He listened as the Rio Kid described several of the outlaws, Robbers' Roost, and made his accusations.

Plummer made notes, and prepared to call his deputies. Sanders, Williams, Biedler and the Rio Kid left the office, and strolled over to the Bearcat, the big saloon where Pryor had told Adam Byrne to meet him.

Several customers were in the Bearcat, a big place with sawdust on the plank floor, and four wood-burning stoves. A dancehall was at one side, while gaming rooms were in the rear, although it was too early in the

85

day for much except drinking, which went on before breakfast and continued until after bedtime. The saloons were useful as meeting-places, where business could be transacted.

Adam Byrne stood at the long bar with the usual mirror behind it. Three aproned barkeeps were on duty. Byrne was grinning as he listened to a smiling red-bearded giant with whom he was drinking and chatting.

"Hello, Bob!" sang out Byrne. "Want you to meet Mr. Fairweather, the discoverer of Alder Gulch."

" 'Old Bill' to friends," the big man said jovially.

There was nothing old about him, however. He was still in his twenties, six-feet-two of bone and sinew. His thick auburn hair curled over his wide shoulders, and his sweeping mustaches and beard glinted with reddish lights.

The three men with the Rio Kid were well-acquainted with William Fairweather, the rollicking discoverer of the great gold strike. He had made a big fortune when a chance whim of Fate had rocketed him from poverty and obscurity to riches and fame. Now he was busy spending it as fast as he could.

The Rio Kid shook hands and let Fairweather buy a drink.

"How'd yuh happen to hit it, Bill?" he inquired, as they drank.

"Oh, me'n some of the boys were out scratchin' in the criks one day," explained Fairweather, "and we was busted, havin' been robbed by Injuns. One mornin' I says to Harry Edgar, my pard, 'Go see if yuh can pan out tobacco money, Ed, and we'll pack up and go back to town.' Dogged if he didn't hit pay dirt as thick as curds in buttermilk! And that was it."

"Bill's promised to take me out prospectin'," Byrne said. "We're startin' in the morning."

"Yuh're a fine lad, Adam," Fairweather said fraternally. "Come on out and I'll show yuh what yuh need to buy to be a miner."

The Rio Kid was satisfied to have Byrne off his hands. He had highly important work himself. For a time he talked with Sanders, Williams and Biedler on plans to rout the Innocents.

"They're mighty powerful," Sanders said. "What we need is to rouse the miners. It *must* be done, before we can wipe the bandits out."

The Rio Kid remained in the Bearcat after his three new acquaintances left, doing some heavy thinking for himself. He wanted to smash the Innocents and make safe the people of the Gulch and of Jefferson. But foremost of all was his secret mission, assigned by Abraham Lincoln himself. He had to locate George Carter and take him. Now that he knew where the big cache of gold was, he hoped to trap the Confederate agent through it. If not, he would pick him up at Robbers' Roost when Carter met Helm again.

He picked up the cool glass, half filled with red whiskey, idly turning it in his slim hand as he ruminated on what his next move must be. Suddenly he became aware that eight or ten men had sifted into the saloon. From the corner of his eyes he watched them in the big mirror. They seemed no more interested in him than they were in a dozen other customers present. The Bearcat was a popular spot, and noon was at hand. Gamblers who had just arisen, clerks out for the noon-day meal, bummers, citizens of Virginia City and surrounding camps were in the street. Appetites made hearty by mountain air and manual toil were sharp and capacious, and everyone seemed intent on the search for food.

Preoccupied with his thoughts, the Rio Kid nearly lost his life because of this absorption. He was off guard for a moment, dangerous in such a place and for such a man. But only for that one breath of space was he not his usual alert self, for the next instant he saw the sinewy, bearded fellow who slouched at the rear door, a double-barreled, sawed-off shot gun under his arm.

Instantly the Rio Kid recognized the cut of the man's whiskers. It was the cut that marked the Innocents and so was the flat knot in the kerchief. Pryor's swift eyes checked three more men with patterned beards entering from the dancehall. Others covered the front exit. In the few moments the Rio Kid had been abstracted those men had casually set themselves so that there would be no way out of the Bearcat without running a gauntlet of point-blank guns.

"Now what —" the Rio Kid thought, the hair tingling at the nape of his neck. The newly healed wound over his ribs itched frantically, as a warning from his central nervous system twitching his skin.

He had not turned around. The moment he did they would cut loose, he was certain. He had to think with the speed of light, and draw his decisions instantly. There was no time to wonder how such a situation had come about.

Only one thing was sure — they were after

him! And he dared not wait to take some action until they were set, until their guns were rising. There were too many of them — and placed in too many directions!

CHAPTER IX
ATTACK IN FORCE

Customers were bending their elbows at either side of the Rio Kid as he became aware of the deadly peril surrounding him. The bar interposed on the fourth side. All the doors were covered and if he ran to a window, the waiting Innocents could cut him down long before he made it.

Glittering eyes were upon him, and one man with a patterned beard gave a slight nod indicating him. There was but one chance, and he seized it. With a swift, lithe movement, he leaped to the top of the bar, and let out a whoop.

"Drinks are on me, gents!" he shouted. "Step up to the bar!"

The astonished customers stared at the sudden apparition dancing on top of the counter.

"Hey, get down off there!" a barkeeper growled.

But free drinks were not to be scorned.

Men who hung around the mining town cadging drinks and free lunch, borrowing an ounce of gold-dust now and then when they could, hastily started toward the Rio Kid.

Even as Pryor turned, apparently hilarious from what he had been drinking, two of the Innocents raised their shotguns, as the eyes of other men in the Bearcat swung on the noisy celebrant. In one quick leap the Rio Kid was down behind the bar. A shotgun bellowed a wink later, the bunched buckshot charge whooshing in the air that an instant before had been occupied by the Rio Kid.

The pellets hit the mirror and glass crashed. Alarmed citizens ducked, trying to get out of the line of fire. A second shotgun roared, cutting splinters off the bar top.

Pryor whipped out an Army Colt and bobbed up. A bearded Innocent was halfway to the bar, gun up to kill, finger ready on trigger. The Rio Kid whipped two shots at the man's head, and the outlaw crashed dead in the sawdust, sliding a yard before he stopped.

Howls of fury arose from the throats of the dead killer's partners, mingling with the alarmed yips of bystanders who wished no part in the sudden melee. Stamping feet shook the floor.

The Rio Kid bobbed up a yard from his first position, and downed a second bandit, whose Colt bullet kicked splinters from the bar. He was hoping they would believe he was dueling it out from back of the long bar, and they did, cursing him, their guns flaming as they forged toward the bar.

Then the Rio Kid made the play he had so swiftly figured out. Stooped over, he ran below the bar toward the rear. Two barkeepers were scrunched down under the counter but they never moved or cried out as his gun menaced them. In a flash he had reached the back end of the bar, where there was a small window. It was closed and glassed, and an iron stove reared in front of it.

Two of his enemies had been standing at the rear entry, which led to the gaming rooms. His ruse had drawn one of them toward the bar. The other was looking up and down the bar for him. The hubbub, yells and cursing, stamping boots, covered the slight noises he made.

The only man who would be dangerous to him at the instant he needed in which to escape, was the Innocent still at the entrance to the gaming room. Without hesitation he threw a bullet into that killer's body, the slug whipping the outlaw around. The Rio Kid had a glimpse of a bearded, twisted face as the outlaw staggered, his gun exploding in unnerved fingers, the bullet digging harmlessly into the floor.

"There he goes, boys!" shrieked the leader of the gang. "Get him, the killer!"

They were spinning around toward him as he skidded behind the high, pot-bellied stove with its glowing, red-hot bowl. His Colt barrel rapped the window glass, shattering it. Bullets and buckshot began hitting the stove. A hail of hot metal fragments burned him, and one ricocheting slug cut a slice out of his upper left arm.

He shot back once, but did not take aim in his haste to dive out the broken window in the breath of time he had made for himself. For an instant the stove protected him from the deadly fire. His attackers rushed in, to find an angle from which to take him, but his spurred boots disappeared over the sill, and the killers' lead only drove into the wood or the wall.

Knowing he had but a couple of seconds in which to make the alley and turn, the Rio Kid dashed for the corner. He was around it before an Innocent stuck his shotgun out the shattered window and fired.

As he ran along Tin Can Alley, yells came from the Bearcat.

"Out and after him, yuh fools!" a man kept bellowing.

Saber was near Sanders' office. But the Rio Kid was cut off from that direction because his back would be toward the back doors and windows of the Bearcat, and the outlaws would certainly rush out that way. As he turned to look back, one of them did leap out the door. He snapped a bullet back, and another bullet replied, shrieking over his head.

Then he saw the jail, and the closed alley door marked *Sheriff.* With a triumphant feeling of relief, the Rio Kid leaped for it, turned the knob, then he was inside out of gunshot.

He shot the bolt over and ran lightly along a corridor past the lockup cells to the office. Sheriff Plummer was standing at the front window, looking toward the Bearcat, as Pryor came through the rear door. A grin spread over the Kid's face. He would have help now, Plummer was known to be an unusually fast man with a gun.

"Well, Ned, did you —" began the sheriff, then he turned and saw the Rio Kid, gun in hand.

He blinked, apparently much surprised.

The Rio Kid slid his Colt back into its holster.

"A bunch of the Innocents tried for me just now in the Bearcat, Sheriff," he said quickly. "They're comin' up the road now."

"I thought you were Ned Ray, my deputy," Plummer said slowly, watching him.

The man at the rear door of the Bearcat had seen the Rio Kid plunge through the back door of the jail. Thumpings began on that alley door and muffled yells of "Killer! Killer!" Some of the pursuers started around to the front, and the Rio Kid stood with his back to the wall.

"Sheriff," he said, wanting to keep the record straight, "I was havin' a snifter at the Bearcat when eight or ten outlaws come in and started surroundin' me. I reckon they musta seen me come in here with Sanders and them other two and report to yuh, or mebbe they didn't like me bein' in Sanders' company. Anyway, I made a break, they opened up, and I shot it out with 'em."

Angry cries came from the front, and the door partially opened.

"Hey, Plummer!" demanded a gruff voice. "You in there?"

"Yes, here I am," the sheriff replied quietly. "What do you want, Vern?"

"A two-gun son just shot three men in

cold blood at the Bearcat! He run in yore back door. He must be hidin' inside."

"He's here," Plummer answered.

The man jumped rapidly aside, out of sight. Others began yelling:

"Fetch him out and string him up!"

"Arrest him, Plummer — he's a desperate man!"

"Take his guns!"

Plummer went to the door, and spoke through the crack.

"What happened, gentlemen?" he inquired.

"Why, that fool got full of red-eye and started to kill everybody in sight!" reported one of Pryor's enemies.

Most of the customers in the saloon who had been witnesses had not known what was going on. They had seen an apparent madman leap to the bar and begin shooting.

"He kilt three men and wounded two more!" an aggrieved voice called. "There wasn't no sense to it."

"They were ambushin' me, Plummer," insisted Pryor.

"You men wait outside," ordered the sheriff.

He shut the door and turned to the Rio Kid, a frown creasing his intelligent brow.

"No doubt your story is the truth, Pryor,"

he said easily. "But I believe in legal means, sir. I'll have to arrest you, but it will only be a formality. I'll lock you up and they can't get at you. Unbuckle your gun-belt and hand it over."

The Rio Kid hesitated. His hand dropped to his belt buckle, but then he shook his head.

"I took note of yore cells back there, Sheriff. They ain't strong and neither are the jail walls. Listen to that!"

"Lynch him — lynch that sidewinder!"

"Who's got a pole for a polecat?"

"Fetch a rope!"

"Murder!"

Mob violence was blowing up, fanned by the foes of the Rio Kid.

"I'll protect you," Plummer promised, but again the Rio Kid shook his head.

"I hate to buck the law, Plummer," he said. "It ain't my style. I'm with yuh against the Innocents. Let me keep my guns, at least."

"I can't do that," the sheriff said flatly. "You're accused of murder, and are under arrest. Let your guns drop and step back."

But the Rio Kid had made up his mind. Stamping feet, raucous yells and threats from outside settled things for him.

"I'll help yuh hold the jail, Plummer," he

offered. "They'll storm us in a minute."

"Fetch him out — run him up, the dog!" a man bawled through the window.

Glass shattered. A gun was thrust through hastily and aimed at the Rio Kid, standing with his back to the wall. He whipped up his Colt, sidestepping as the slug drilled the wooden wall. His answer burned the gunman's cheek and the fellow dropped with a yip. Roars of fury echoed from outside.

Plummer's eyes snapped. He was angry.

"Easy, Sheriff," the Rio Kid drawled. "I can see yore point, and yuh'll hafta listen to their story. But as I told yuh —"

Plummer's left hand blurred, streaking to his revolver. He was fast, but the Rio Kid shaded him. Again the Army Colt whipped to position, pinning the sheriff where he was, with his weapon half out of its holster.

"Don't make me shoot," begged the Rio Kid. "I don't want to hurt yuh, Plummer."

Henry Plummer carefully opened his fingers and his Colt slid back into place.

"All right," he said after a moment. "You killed three men and wounded others. I believed you when you said you meant to help me trap the outlaws. But this is not the way to do it. I don't believe in anarchy."

"Yuh call self-defense anarchy?" demanded Pryor. "I tell yuh they come up on me without warnin'."

Plummer shrugged coldly. He was angry, and ruffled at having been beaten to the draw. He sat down in his chair and stared at the Rio Kid.

"Before I hurt my right arm," he muttered, "you couldn't have done it."

CHAPTER X
ON THE DODGE

Bob Pryor thought fast. With the sheriff suspicious of him, with so many citizens seeing the fight in the wrong way, he was in the utmost danger.

The men of Alder Gulch, once aroused, were not the sort to show patience. He could not remain forever in the jail, not with the sheriff against him. He was unknown, and the Innocents were powerful, in force.

Wood splintered loudly from the rear of the jailhouse. They were breaking down the door in the alley. Heavy footsteps pounded in the hall, and the desperate Pryor pressed against the wall, watching doors and windows as well as he could, and with the sheriff glowering at him.

Abruptly then, from the corridor, a commanding voice that gave the Rio Kid new hope rang out:

"Throw up yore hands, gents!"

"Williams!" the Rio Kid shouted, for he

had recognized the voice of James Williams, Sanders' friend.

The next moment Sanders himself was calling:

"Pryor, Pryor! Quick — this way!"

He leaped through the open door and ran to the back of the jail. Sanders, Williams, Biedler and three other heavily armed men were there, with a dozen or more of the quickly formed mob lined against the cell bars.

Sanders seized the Rio Kid's arm.

"Your horse is waiting two doors down. Ride for it! We can hold 'em for a few minutes."

The determined vigilantes kept the mob at bay. Two remained inside, guarding the simmering citizens there. The rest, with Williams and Sanders in the lead, formed around the Rio Kid and ran him out into Tin Can Alley.

Guns bristled from the circle of protectors as they hustled toward Saber who was dancing impatiently in the meantime.

"What's the idea?" a bearded Innocent bawled. "Hand that killer over!"

But it was over too swiftly for the mob to get into action, and besides, most of them were in front of the jail. The Rio Kid grinned as he hit leather, raising a hand to thank Sanders and Williams.

"I'll be in touch with yuh," he promised. "Them men who was gunnin' for me at the Bearcat were Innocents."

"We savvy that," growled Williams. "Get goin'."

The Rio Kid spurted off between two stables, and cut up the beaten lane behind the buildings. Men began running through the alley hunting him. Catcalls and wild bullets sped in his wake as, low over the dun, he cantered off.

He splashed across the creek, the frozen edges crackling under the horse's hoofs, and dashed up the slope through stunted brush and trees bare of foliage. Horsemen set out to pursue him but he showed them a flash of Saber's speed, reaching the ridge road and putting distance between Virginia City and himself.

Out of sight behind rises and dips, and patches of firs, the Rio Kid found a beaten trail and he took it. He used every trick and clever method known to scouts to hide his sign. He had been born in Apache country in Texas, had stalked Indians and kept out of their way since he had been big enough to hold up a rifle.

In the lee of many bluffs, he knew, there would be loose shale that did not retain definite marks, and snow did not collect on the windward sides. Water, too, could conceal his passage.

Making the higher mountains, he paused to look back for pursuit. Far down the main gulch he saw parties of riders. He had made several false feints in that direction in his doubling back and forth, and they had jumped the wrong way after reaching one of his dead-end trails.

The jolting had started his wounded arm to bleeding profusely, and the cold made his face red and raw, burned his eyes and nostrils. He tried to bind his injury, to stanch the flow, but it was clumsy working with only one hand and a strip of undershirt he tore off.

"I'll hafta reach shelter by night," he muttered, wondering where that would be, for he was a fugitive, from the law of Alder Gulch as well as from the lawless.

The sheriff would arrest him if he got a chance, and there were plenty of witnesses to swear that the Rio Kid had murdered three men at the saloon, if he got as far as a trial. Moreover, any Innocent would shoot him on sight, and that was their evident intention, from the determined way they started after him. He had time now to wonder about that attack at the Bearcat.

So far as he knew, none of the outlaws had ever had a good enough look at him to have at once recognized him there.

Up in the hills the wind cut like a sharp knife. The Rio Kid had not entirely recovered from the terrible wound he had taken at Gettysburg, and the hurt in his arm and the strain of fighting were telling on him. He needed help. Sanders would certainly help him, but that meant riding back to Virginia City — and that he could not do. Besides, it was possible that Sanders, Biedler, and Williams would make themselves scarce for a time, since they had openly abetted his escape.

South ranged the Tobacco Roots, and in the gap between that range and the Ruby Mountains ran the Great Salt Lake Road. Far to the north showed the bluish, snow-clad tops of the McCarty Mountains. All of them were subsidiary ranges of the Bitter Roots, the dominating Continental Divide.

Streams cut deep ravines through the brooding hills — the Grasshopper, Alder Creek, Big Hole, Passamari, Jefferson River, and others. Small settlements and ranches nestled in sheltered vales. But nowhere could the Rio Kid ask for refuge. He was on the dodge and could trust no stranger.

"After dark," he muttered to Saber, "we'll

head for the Robertses. They'll take care of us."

He began hunting a way by which he could reach the settlement of Jefferson, but miners were at work everywhere along the streams, and the towns were crowded. Robbers' Roost lay not so many miles off, but in his weakened condition he did not wish to go there, even in disguise.

"I'll be there Tuesday night, though," he thought. "When Carter and Helm meet again."

All through the afternoon he kept moving. When the sun, huge and red, touched the summits of the Bitter Roots that evening he was nearly done in. He was still losing blood, and was far out in the mountains. The dun was tired, too, and stiffened from the cold wind. Before he could find the trail to Alder Gulch and Jefferson, dark fell. He moved slowly, fighting the weakness and lethargy that stole upon him.

At last he had to stop and rest. He pulled up under a great rock bluff overhanging the trail and tried to unlimber his muscles, but his head was swimming, and he could not get warm. After a time he remounted and went on, with no idea of how near danger was to him again.

It was the dun who saved him. The beast

rippled his black stripe and sniffed uneasily. The Rio Kid stopped at once, peering ahead in the blackness. Faintly he heard men's voices.

"If he comes this way," one of them was saying, "I'll shoot his eyes out! Anyway, Boone'll track him down tomorrer."

"It's cold settin' here," another grumbled. "What's the use wastin' all this good time on one lobo like the Rio Kid? We can get him if he dares show in these parts agin."

"The Chief says we're to hold this road," the other man told him, "and we're holdin' it."

"That's right," a third chimed in. "Obey orders. Yuh learn that in the Army."

"What Army?" asked a fourth derisively. "When the War broke out so did you, Dutch."

"Aw, shut up," the accented, thick voice snarled. "You got a yeller stripe down yore own spine, Lane."

Wearily the Rio Kid turned the dun and softly retraced his course. He had not seen the speakers. They were hidden down on the road, watching the turn, and in his present condition he could not even fight his way past them.

A couple of miles back, he knew he could go no farther. Falling from the saddle, he managed to undo the cinches so that Saber would be free. He unrolled his blanket and wrapped in it.

"Don't go so far, Saber, old boy," he whispered.

In some rocks he found a partially dry spot and curled up to sleep. There was no dry firewood near and anyway he dared not beacon his position to his foes.

It was an uneasy rest. The cold penetrated to the marrow, and the wind howled about the jagged mountain tops. The stars and slice of moon, obscured from time to time by scudding clouds, were wintry.

The first touch of gray over the Tobacco Roots found him numb, unable to move. His head was light and he fought against delirium with all his remaining power.

But the sapping wounds were stronger.

Nightmare visions began driving through his mind. Suddenly the crash of cannon burst in his beating eardrums, and he was at Gettysburg, on the sleek, swift Saber, charging at the head of his troop, saber raised. Before him the handsome, reckless figure of George A. Custer, his general.

"At 'em, boys, give 'em hell!" Bob Pryor thought he shouted, although only a whisper came from his cracked lips.

After a while he quieted. The fight was

over. A pair of deep eyes, sad but kind, watched him. The face became delineated, gaunt and anxious, framed by dark chin whiskers and hair.

"Lincoln," he gasped. "President Lincoln! "How — how did you get here?"

Faint and yet clear, sentences beat in his brain.

"Fourscore and seven years ago our fathers brought forth . . . a new Nation. . . . All men are created equal. . . . The brave men, living and dead, who struggled here. . . . The world will little note nor long remember what we say here, but it can never forget what they did. . . . That government of the people, by the people, for the people, shall not perish from the earth. . . ."

The Rio Kid tried to get to his feet.

"I'm counting on you, Captain Pryor," Lincoln said.

"I'll carry it through!"

A starshell burst in the Rio Kid's fancy and he was quiet, slumped in a heap, the blanket off.

CHAPTER XI
PROSPECTING

Adam Byrne jogged along on his mule, with the cheerful chatter of "Old Bill" Fairweather, whose long legs almost touched the ground on either side of his burro, in his ears. The giant, rich as any man in the gold fields, had, true to his promise, been ready at daybreak to accompany Byrne into the mountains and show him how to hunt gold, despite the fact that Fairweather had enjoyed a big night in Virginia City. Fairweather was a real prospector, in it for the thrill and gamble. He was in his glory now as the two rode along, with a third mule behind them carrying their packs, grub and tools. Round pans glistened in the new light, pans they would use to wash out the sands of streams.

"You got to have a nose for goldminin', boy," rumbled Fairweather, nodding his shaggy head, "as well as eyes that can see through rock, dirt and water. Never say die, either. Yuh might hunt for years and find not even tobacco money, but the next day hit it. Greatest sport in the world, huntin' gold."

"I don't know much about it," Byrne replied. "I've spent the last three years soldierin', Bill."

"That ain't bad either, but it ain't as dangerous. Leastways yuh savvy who yore enemy is. Here yuh don't."

"You mean road-agents?"

"Them, and other things, like Injuns — some anyways. And cold and hunger and thirst and other things I could mention."

The sun was coming up bright and yellow, over the Tobacco Roots behind them. They had ridden several miles from Virginia City and Alder Gulch on a winding trail.

Byrne was deeply worried over his friend, the Rio Kid, who had got himself in to tall trouble the day before at the Bearcat. Byrne had heard the shooting, and had seen the mob, but had not known who was causing the commotion until long after Pryor had escaped up Tin Can Alley and made the mountains.

Byrne and Fairweather had come from the store, where they had been purchasing a small outfit, and had watched the organizing of the chase.

111

"There go Sanders and Williams," Bill had muttered. "Looks like they ain't so popular, Adam."

A knot of men, Sanders' friends, had ridden off, with menacing rifles protruding from the group. The mob had not wished to tangle with such a determined force, and had disappeared up the Gulch road.

Byrne had noticed that Saber was gone, and listening as Fairweather inquired about the rumpus, he had learned, with a shock, that the fugitive the Virginia City men honed to lynch was none other than his comrade, the Rio Kid.

Sanders and his friends had not shown up that evening. Nor had Pryor been seen. Plummer's office had buzzed with activity, men slipping in and out to report on the progress of the chase.

Byrne finally had dropped off to sleep. But when he and Fairweather had started off this morning they had learned the Rio Kid was still at large.

Up in the mountains, Fairweather finally came upon a spot he liked. They dismounted, and after Bill had taken a long drink from his whiskey bottle, they went to work. A feeder stream rushed through a rocky bed to join Alder Creek below, and Fairweather pointed to some brilliant pinspots of yellow in the sandy sides.

"Scoop it up, boy," he ordered.

It was the crudest sort of placer mining, but Byrne quickly learned how to load the pan with dirt, slosh in water, and with circular wrist motion float off the lighter materials. Gold particles, being heavier, would sink to the bottom of the wet mess, although sometimes small fragments were often lost over the side.

"Color!" cried Old Bill, pointing to three tiny specks in the bottom of the pan. "Git yore pick and dig into the side of that hill, Adam boy! Mebbe we'll hit the mother lode."

With great enthusiasm, Byrne went to work. His pick drove deep into rotten quartz, and brought it down in chunks and sliding gravel. It was back-breaking toil. They shoveled it and broke it up and, taking panfuls to the brook, washed and washed.

At first they picked out a trace or two of color. Then they made twelve essays without a sign of gold.

"Don't look so good, after all, Adam," grunted Fairweather after a couple of hours of this. "Mebbe we better try another spot. But don't be downhearted. The next place may be it."

The sun was quite warm as they moved on and the work had brought sweat out on Adam Byrne, who led the pack-mule. They circled around, and came to a stony gulch, with a southern exposure to its steplike ledges.

"Dig there!" ordered Fairweather.

Byrne set to work again. He cut away some loose stuff, hoping to find a fortune in gold, and exposed a cleft in the stone, a dark slit into which the sun pierced but a few feet.

"Whir — whir — whir!"

The sound meant nothing to Byrne, who had been brought up on a Pennsylvania farm. Then he glimpsed a slowly rising serpent's head. He recoiled in alarm, knowing he must have dug out a den of hibernating rattlers.

"Look out, Bill — snakes!" he cried.

Fairweather had had several large swallows from his bottle, and was in high spirits. He stepped around Byrne and plunged his arm down into the cleft.

"Bill, are you crazy!" shouted Byrne.

Fairweather's hand appeared, clutching a mess of rattlesnakes. They were sluggish from the cold but slowly were wrapping themselves around his bare arm. Forked tongues shot out, and the dry-pod whirring was louder.

"They'll never bite me," explained Fairweather, "not even when it's hot. I can play Yankee Doodle with 'em."

Laughing, he put the big snakes back in their nest.

"Suppose we dig somewhere else?" suggested Byrne, and his companion was willing.

An hour later Fairweather pulled up, looking down across the wooded dip.

"There's a loose hoss, Adam boy," he said. "He's winded us, and — huh! He's comin' up. That's queer. Mustang, too."

Byrne glanced the way Fairweather pointed — and gasped.

"Saber!" he exclaimed. "That's Saber, the Rio Kid's horse, Bill!"

"The Rio Kid? Eh, you mean that hombre who kilt the men in Virginia City yestiddy. Wonder how come that dun got loose?"

Saber came rushing at them up the slope, his teeth bared. He snorted, and stamped, but when Byrne tried to catch hold of his mane, he threatened to bite and backed off.

He kept running toward them, then back.

"He wants us to come with him, I reckon," Byrne growled.

"Oh, shucks," said Fairweather. "We got enough to worry us without takin' any lip

115

from a cayuse."

But Byrne was not in the mood to jest. He followed Saber and kept on going as the dun would dash off, then look back. Fairweather shrugged, but also came along.

A mile away, the mouse-colored mustang stopped beside some rocks. Byrne dismounted when Saber did not keep on going but danced about restlessly, whinnying. And in the boulders Byrne found the stiff form of the Rio Kid!

Byrne believed his friend was dead, but Fairweather did not. The prospector had seen men in the extreme of exposure before.

"He's near froze," he declared, "but we'll thaw him out, Adam boy. See that there incurvin' boulder beyond? Build up a fire there. Yuh'll find some dry enough sticks from that there dead spruce. This here wound this hombre's got has drained a lot of blood outa him. Lucky we got Valley Tan to spare. That's the best redeye there is. It'll build a fire inside him."

Byrne soon had a blaze going to the concave face of rock, and they laid the Rio Kid on a blanket and covered him with another, so that the heat was reflected on him from its surface. Old Bill — who wasn't any older than Byrne or the Rio Kid — poured a large gulp of liquor between the bluish lips of the unconscious man. He examined the wound in Pryor's left arm. It had clotted and the bleeding had stopped, so he washed it and bound it up.

It was an hour before the Rio Kid began to stir and mutter. But when he opened his eyes they were wild, and his talk was incoherent.

"Lincoln!" he gasped. "Lincoln — Look out for them flankers, Sergeant! Spread 'em to the left more — Fourscore and seven years ago —"

"He's shore spoutin'," Fairweather said. "His heart's as strong as a hoss', though. He'll pull through. We need to get him to shelter as soon as possible. The damp ain't none too good for him. Reckon we'll jack him up and run him to Virginia City."

"We will not!" exploded Adam Byrne. "Why, they'd string him higher'n a kite there, Bill — you know that! No, we've got to figure a better place for him to hide out. I know — Jefferson! The folks there'll do anything for him."

"Jefferson?" repeated Fairweather, puzzled. "Why, there's a passel of Rebels there, ain't there? Gen'ral Roberts and all? This feller fit on the other side."

"They're the best people I ever met," Byrne growled. "They're Americans just like us, Bill. They think they're right and they've fought for it. One of us has got to head there and fetch help. I don't know these trails so well."

"I'll go," Fairweather said. "You stick here, Adam boy, and keep feedin' him swigs of mountain dew. It'll make him sit up and sing treble 'fore yuh know it. Hold him down though if he tries to rise up and the fight the Rebs. He's de-leerious."

CHAPTER XII
TO THE RESCUE

Old Bill Fairweather, an original explorer and prospector in the district, saddled his mule and started down the mountain. Byrne remained close to the Rio Kid, keeping him warm and feeding him Valley Tan. Three hours passed. Byrne hoped that Fairweather would get back before it was dark, with help from Jefferson.

The Rio Kid had quieted down and was sleeping well, though now and then he would stir and mutter incoherent sentences.

The young lieutenant kept up the fire. Some of the wood he managed to find and break up into logs with his ax was soggy and gave off great volumes of smoke which drifted high into the afternoon sky. He had not thought of that as bringing danger, and was squatted by his friend's head, when suddenly a strident, snarling voice called:

"Hey, you! What's up?"

Startled, Byrne swung, looking over his

shoulder. Half a dozen men in rough clothing, whose beards were cut to an identical
pattern, and with bandannas tied in flat
sailor's knots, were sitting their horses,
watching him from across the rocks.

One of them, a tall, angular fellow, with
black, fiery eyes, and a snarling mouth, was
Boone Helm, though Byrne had no idea of
the man's identity. However, he did know
of the Innocents, from what he had heard
the Rio Kid and Roberts saying, and
guessed that these heavily armed men were
some of the gang. Apparently none of them
suspected they had ever seen Byrne before,
for the young lieutenant was wearing different clothing from what he had worn on the
trail when the outlaws had struck Roberts'
pack-train.

"Seen your smoke and wondered who it
was," rasped on Helm. "Prospectin', are
yuh? Any luck?"

"No, not yet."

"We were lookin' for a man on a dun,
feller known as the Rio Kid," Helm went
on. "Seen Old Bill Fairweather earlier and
he said nobody was up here. Then we
caught the smoke in the sky and . . . say,
who's in that there blanket?"

He had sighted the muffled Rio Kid, who
had stirred uneasily. Off to the right and,

glancing that way, Helm saw Saber, grazing in a small niche.

Byrne caught the fiery glint in the outlaw chief's sunken eyes. The irises of Helm's eyes were as black as ink but the whites were so inflamed that the impression was that his eyes were red.

Helm cursed, throwing a bony hand to his Navy .44 revolver. Byrne knew he had recognized the dun, and had guessed that the man in the blanket roll was the elusive scout they were seeking. Adam was squatted down in front of his friend, and the rocks gave them both some protection.

Reaching for his Army Colt, he fired a quick shot ahead of Helm. The bullet burned the hide of the bandit leader's mustang, causing him to leap about madly, and Helm's shot missed by feet as he fought his careening horse. Byrne let go a second one which punctured Helm's flat black hat. Then he threw himself down in front of Pryor as five more Innocents, behind Helm, opened fire.

Bullets spattered into the curving face of the big rock. But the ground sloped, and the Innocents were unable to reach Byrne without coming up so close that he could shoot them. Byrne hit one fellow who tried it, and sent him back with a smashed arm, swearing a blue streak.

"Get back, boys!" Boone Helm shouted. "We got 'em! They can't get away! Soon as it's dark we'll take 'em. We'll carve 'em bit by bit when we catch 'em."

The Innocents began shooting at Saber then. But as the dun felt the close whine of lead, he moved away. They were unable to catch him.

Byrne spent anxious hours. It was a question whether darkness would fall before help could reach them. He overheard Boone Helm ordering one of his high-graders to ride to "camp" and fetch more Innocents.

The sun dropped behind the Bitter Roots. Gorgeous streamers of light came from the mountains, reflecting in the sky — purple and gold, light-blue, green.

The night was close at hand when shouts sounded from below, and with a thrill of relief Byrne recognized Fairweather's voice. Helm and his men went down the trail a short distance, but returned and began blasting the curving rock with bullets, hoping to get the two sheltered there with ricochets.

A quarter of an hour later, as Byrne dueled it out with them, Fairweather, Taze Roberts, Ben Lee and three more young men from Jefferson charged up, guns in hand.

Helm drew off as they approached, hurling back threats and challenges.

"Yuh'll, pay for this," he howled in mad fury. "Yuh're pertectin' a fugitive from the law! The sheriff wants that Rio Kid sidewinder."

"Come on and try to take him!" shouted Taze Roberts.

But the Innocents would not face the determined men from Jefferson. Long-distance shots pattered harmlessly in the rocks and dirt as the rescuers placed Pryor on an improvised stretcher held between two horses, and started off with him, a rear guard keeping Helm at bay.

When night came, they were halfway down the mountain on the way back to Jefferson. Their enemies were behind, but dared not approach too closely without reinforcements. . . .

The Rio Kid came back to himself with a terrific start.

It took him some moments to identify his surroundings. He was lying on a cot, and a fire burned warmly on a hearth. Low voices came to him, and he saw

Adam Byrne sitting on a bench near the blaze, beside Dorothy Roberts. Then the furnishings of the room told him that he was in General Roberts' home, at Jefferson.

"Why can't you forget the War?" Byrne was saying in an eager, low voice to the girl. "When it's over, Dorothy, we'll all be Americans again, won't we?"

"It's hard," she murmured. "I lost a brother and two cousins and a mighty big number of friends."

Outside, not far away, in the darkness, a gunshot rang out. The two beside the fire were silent for a moment, then Byrne took the girl's hand, looking earnestly into her eyes.

"I love you, Dorothy," he said in a low voice. "I knew it the first time we met. Your father says I can stay here and help work the claim. Do you want me to?"

"Yes — I wish you would, Adam," she confessed in a soft whisper.

"Byrne!" the Rio Kid called suddenly, and both of them started guiltily.

Adam jumped to his feet and came over, looking down into his friend's drawn face.

"How you feel, Bob?" he asked.

"All right. How'd I get here?"

"Fairweather and I found you up in the

mountains. Your dun led us to you. We fetched you down."

Another shot rang out, and the Rio Kid asked:

"What's that shootin' about?"

Byrne shrugged. "Nothin' much. That Boone Helm devil trailed us in. They tried to take you, but Roberts fought 'em off."

Loud, angry voices were raised outside.

"Hold those guns, Roberts!" a man cried. "You're shootin' at the law!"

"Well, Plummer, what do you want?" demanded the general, who was out in the darkness protecting the settlement.

"I want that fugitive you're harborin', known as the Rio Kid, and I want him tonight," Henry Plummer's cold tones insisted.

"You can't have him," replied General Roberts. "He's a guest of ours, Plummer, and we won't let you take him."

The flickering flames of the fire danced merrily.

The Rio Kid touched his chin with his hand, to find a quarter inch growth of whiskers there. He sat bolt upright.

"What night is this, Adam?" he demanded.

"Thursday," replied Byrne. "Lie back and take it easy. You've been off your head since we brought you in, Bob."

"What time is it?"

"About eight o'clock. The Innocents weren't around this afternoon, but the general kept careful guard, expectin' 'em back tonight. But Plummer's come instead ... Hey, where'd you think you're going?"

"Miss Dorothy, will yuh go fix me some coffee, please!" begged the Rio Kid.

"Yes, surely." She left the room, going to the lean-to.

"Keep her outside, till I'm dressed," ordered the Rio Kid. "Where's my saddle-bags?"

"In the shed."

"Fetch 'em in, will yuh?"

When Byrne brought the saddle-bags the Rio Kid put on the torn gray trousers and jacket, the rig Taze Roberts had given him. He smeared some charcoal from a log on his unshaven face, and Dorothy brought him in a steaming hot drink. It braced him.

"I got to ride, Adam, and now," he said grimly. "Will yuh saddle up Saber for me, and hold him out there in the shadows?"

"Aw, Bob, you're not in shape to ride now," Byrne began to protest, but the command in his friend's eyes was that of a superior officer.

Byrne subsided, leaving by the back door. The Rio Kid found his pistols and belts hanging on a peg in the lean-to, and strapped them on under his coat. As he was finishing these swift preparations, General Roberts came through the front door, a troubled look on his bearded face.

He started as he saw the Rio Kid.

"Why, Captain Pryor! I hardly knew you. You — you look like a Confederate guerrilla. You're feelin' better, suh?"

"Fine, and many thanks for yore help. Where's Plummer?"

"He's ridden off, but threatens to be back in force and arrest us all for harborin' —" Roberts broke off. He did not wish to hurt his guest's feelings.

"I know all about it. When he returns, General, I'll be gone. I'm leavin' now."

"You're welcome here, Captain."

"I know it. Stay on yore guard, Roberts. Yuh'll hear from me pronto."

Armed men circled the little settlement, on the alert. Byrne had Saber ready and the Rio Kid clinched leather, himself again. He passed through the line and took the steep path, full-tilt, for Robbers' Roost.

But swift as the dun was, it was well after nine o'clock before Pryor sighted the blinking windows of the saloon rendezvous of the Innocents.

In the night, all cats are gray — and so

are most horses. Though aware that the Innocents knew Saber was the Rio Kid's horse, he did not mean to let them have a close view of his mount.

He could have ridden another horse, of course, but he felt he needed the dun's speed and uncanny knowledge to carry him through on his perilous mission.

CHAPTER XIII
THE MEETING

Saddled mustangs, twenty or more of them, were bunched together outside Robbers' Roost. As before, the Rio Kid left Saber at the rear corner, in the dark shadows, and reeled around to the front entrance. Shrilly whistling "Dixie" he staggered inside, and without looking about, went to the bar.

"Valley Tan, and a toast to Jeff Davis!" he shouted, banging on the top of the crude bar.

All eyes turned upon him. They saw the round-shouldered, unsteady figure in gray, the whiskered face and black dirt stains, and a snicker ran around the saloon. Belligerency gone, they prepared to bait him. A number of the Innocents were in the place, but Pryor did not see Boone Helm and Carter.

"Why, it's Johnny Reb hisself," the baldheaded proprietor, Skinner, remarked jovially. "Spend that Confederate money yet, bummer? Where yuh been keepin' yoreself?"

"There," growled the Rio Kid, throwing down a small gold nugget.

"Oh, prospectin', huh? Too bad yuh can't stake a claim in a whiskey distillery."

The jest brought a roar of laughter.

"Three cheers for Abe Lincoln!" one of the Innocents proclaimed derisively, to infuriate the supposed Rebel partisan.

"Who said that?" The "bummer's" bleary eyes scowled down the line. Smudges of charcoal distorted his features.

"I did!" a chicken-necked desperado growled. "What about it? If yuh want to spout, let's have a tune, Johnny Reb." The fellow yanked out a Navy pistol and fired a shot that burrowed in the flooring an inch from Pryor's toe.

The Rio Kid blinked, feigning fear, and began to sing "Dixie."

"Not that Rebel yell!" growled the baiter. "Make it Yankee Doodle!"

The Rio Kid obliged.

"Terrible," snarled the Innocent. "Dance, blast yuh, for singin' so bad."

Bullets rapped the boards and Pryor did an uneven dance down the room. He collapsed at the back, sinking into a chair close to the rear partition, and all laughed as he closed his eyes and began to snore. As their raucous yells quieted, he caught Helm's snarl from the other side of the partition, as he had hoped he would.

"Course yuh can trust me, Carter. We've worked together before, ain't we?"

"This is a big one, Boone. Tell yore chief this, and let's have it above-board, no hard feelin's. I have a list of sixty men who work for him and you, practically all the road-agents from Bannack to Virginia City, savvy — and the proof against 'em that goes with it."

"Where is it?" asked Helm instantly.

Carter gave a short laugh. "Never mind. But I promise yuh this, Boone. If anything goes sour on this job, the list will be in the proper hands."

"Yuh mean the sheriff?"

Carter laughed again.

"Do you take me for a fool? I'm a desperate man, Boone. I mean to pay yuh as agreed, but I take no unnecessary chances. That bullion goes through to the South. I was thinkin' of Wilbur Sanders. Every man on that list will stretch hemp if Sanders gets his paws on it — as he will, if things don't go right. I don't cotton to Sanders or any other Yankee, but I have to pertect myself. That's all. Tell yore Chief that, in case he's contemplatin' anything different from what we planned."

There was a silence. Then Helm's chair scraped, and he said, "All right," in a strangled voice. Plainly he was holding in his anger.

The Rio Kid had missed most of this talk between Carter and Helm, but what he had heard had made the perilous chance he had taken worthwhile.

Carter did not enter the saloon, but Helm strode in, went to the bar and downed a full tumbler of raw whiskey. Boone swung, his reddened, furious eyes sweeping the room. They paused a moment on the sleeping, drunken bummer in gray, then flicked his followers, the Innocents.

"All set, gents," he snarled. "Meet the others at the big live-oak beyond the branch, savvy? I'll be along within two hours of the time yuh get there. Now ride."

The Innocents trooped out, gunbelts creaking. Helm drank again, alone, and scowling, stamped outside.

Heavy hoofs pounded the frozen ground. The gang rode off, and the Rebel derelict got up from his chair, evidently disturbed by the stirrings about him. He went unsteadily to the bar, had a drink, paid up, and lurched out, followed by the amused eyes of Skinner, the saloon owner, who, as a secret member of the Wild Bunch, gave them tips on travelers whose purses might be well-filled.

As the Rio Kid went out into the starry night, with the snow crisp underfoot, he saw a solitary horseman turning onto a narrow trail that led in the general direction of Alder Gulch. It was Boone Helm.

Picking up Saber — he had to be careful, for Carter, the Confederate agent, was still inside the back room — Pryor let his quarry have a head start, then followed.

Before crossing the top of the ridge he dismounted to reconnoiter. Creeping up, he could see Helm against the snow, descending the steep trail to the deep, narrow gulch. Half an hour later, as the Rio Kid followed, Boone Helm hit the main road running through the Gulch proper. He stopped outside a saloon where a hurdy-gurdy was blaring, and yells of celebrants filled the air.

Helm dismounted and walked into the dark side passage. The Rio Kid hurried around the other way and was just in time to hear the door close, halfway up the alley. On tiptoe, he crept nearer.

Partitions and windows were skimpy in the jerry-built structures of Alder Gulch. Though the wind howled in the passage, the Rio Kid, ear to a crack, could catch the voices in there.

"He's suspicious, I tell yuh," Boone Helm insisted. "He's got a list of us, he says, and when I asked would he give it to the sheriff, he laughed — just like he knowed it all, Chief."

"Let him have his rope," another voice said coldly, "and he'll stretch it himself, Helm. I told you to lead him on, and once we get that million out of the warehouse on the road, it's ours. To devil with the Confederacy!"

"I ain't sayin' that, though it does look like they've lost the War. Me, I'm all for linin' our own pockets, but I'm tellin' yuh — Carter's smart."

"He'll look all-fired brilliant with bulletholes in his head, lyin' out for vulture bait," said the other man icily.

"Yeah, but how about that list of us he says he's got?" insisted Helm.

There was another silence. Then the man Helm had called Chief replied:

"A fellow like Carter would never trust such a paper with anyone but himself. I'll bet a hundred ounces against a glass of rotgut he'll have it on him — provided he ain't bluffin'."

"He's onto you all right — and he'll talk, if he has to."

"He'll not be able to talk after Saturday. If Sanders, Williams and Biedler ride with that pack-train guard that's going out Saturday, so much the better. They're tryin' to rouse the miners against us, though they don't savvy about me. But it's a question how long the territory'll be safe for us, Boone, with them on the prod as they are, that's a fact. We'll have to hit first and smash 'em. So far I've blocked every move they've made, because they've let me in on their plans.

"I'm furnishin' twenty of the guards for Saturday, men no one has suspected yet. I'll swear out a warrant for this Carter's arrest, just in case, and give it to Ned Ray. Now we can't afford any slips, savvy? You come to my office in Virginia City at midnight Friday. Come in the back door — I'll see it's unlocked for you — and we can check and recheck every detail then, in case there's any change in Sanders' plans."

"I'll be there," promised Helm.

"What about tonight?" demanded the Chief. "That Rio Kid skunk is still lyin' up at Roberts' camp in Jefferson, and I want no more misses. That bunch is too dangerous to us, with Sanders snoopin' around and questionin' everybody in sight. Roberts has already made complaints to my office against you and a couple of the other boys."

"He'll never squeal again, not after to-night," growled Helm. "Nor will any of 'em. It's all set to wipe 'em out."

The shock of what the Rio Kid was over-hearing was so startling that he could not believe his own ears. And he was sure he knew the voice of the Chief who was talking to Helm.

He heard them moving inside, and squeezed himself against the panels of a door. He was hidden in the blackness of the niche when Boone Helm emerged and swung toward the road. The bandit did not look his way and if he had he probably would not have seen the Rio Kid in the darkness.

The other man in the private room of the saloon came to close the door after his lieutenant. The Rio Kid glimpsed the tall, neatly-clad figure, the clipped mustache, with the lamplight catching the reddish glints in the hairs.

Bits of evidence which had seemed unim-portant coincidences now became vital links in a damning chain. Pryor recalled the mo-ment when he had run into the jail at Virginia City with a mob at his heels, and subsequent happenings which fitted per-fectly with his startling discovery.

For the man called "Chief" by Boone Helm, who was field-gang leader of the murderous Innocents, the man who was the most bare-faced, horrible killer of them all, was Henry Plummer, high sheriff of Virginia City and light of the law in Alder Gulch!

"They are goin' to hit Jefferson tonight," Bob Pryor thought grimly, as he carefully retreated around the saloon, and sought the waiting dun. "They savvy Roberts is on guard, so they must be expectin' to overwhelm the sentries in spite of all."

What he had dug out concerning the hypocritical, thieving Plummer was so important he dared not trust it within his own mind alone for long. If anything happened to him, Plummer would still be safe, unexposed.

The enormity of it was breathtaking. Henry Plummer, posing as the protector of the decent elements, could give vital information to Boone Helm and the Innocents. As sheriff, Plummer would know of gold shipments, of winnings at gambling tables. Complaints would be made at his offices, and he could tip off the road-agents of any danger to their precious hides. The Rio Kid was remembering now how Plummer had been buzzing about importantly when the stage carrying gold bullion had been preparing to leave Virginia City.

"Why, the rascal was up in the hills the day Roberts' pack-train was hit, too!" he growled. "Watchin', I'll bet! I been a fool not to get leery of him 'fore this!"

But so engrossed had he been with bringing George Carter to book, and discovering how gold was making its way from here to the Confederate lines that he had given no time to smelling out Helm's "Chief."

CHAPTER XIV
MURDER

Halting momentarily down the rough main road, the Rio Kid contemplated the mining town, with its red lights and joints where men and their women companions were whooping it up in the night. Oblivious to all but their own immediate pleasures, these citizens had allowed an ulcer to fester in the very heart of their community — the Innocents under Henry Plummer.

Now the men who might have fought them were paralyzed, disunited, afraid to go against such a powerful gang. The trails were unsafe, and a man who made a gold strike, or a lucky winning at faro usually lost his life for it. The clarion call that had been sounded by Colonel Wilbur Sanders went unheeded. The people would not rouse from their lethargy.

As the Rio Kid rode along, signs told him he was in Laurin, a town not far from Virginia City in Alder Gulch.

"I better chance it and take help with me if I can get it," he decided. "Helm savvies Jefferson is ready for him and his men, so he must have a way of overcomin' them Jefferson fellers."

Sanders and Williams were the only men he dared trust, though. He could not ask help in this town, for no doubt the deputies here were men appointed by Henry Plummer. And he could not take a gamble on strangers. He set Saber's head down the Gulch toward Virginia City. He would be only one more gun if he went on to Jefferson alone, and would not make much appreciable difference, since the men of the settlement already knew they might be hit any time.

Twenty minutes swift ride over the frozen road and he crossed the creek into Virginia City. There was a light on in Sanders' office and the blind was drawn, a precaution the colonel was wise to take, since he was known to be an opponent of the Innocents.

Sanders unbolted the door at the Rio Kid's hoarse whisper of identification. He held a horse pistol in one hand.

When he saw the slouched, disreputable figure in gray, with the flat hat and the bearded, dirty face, Sanders drew quickly back, raising his gun with a threatening gesture.

"You're not Captain Pryor," he snarled, eyes blazing. "You Rebel bummer, what's your game?"

"Lemme in, Colonel! Hold yore gun, now. It's me — shore it is."

The Rio Kid stepped under the hanging lamp so that Sanders could look at him closely.

"It is you," Sanders said at last. "I'd never have known you." He looked out the door, craning his neck to make sure Pryor had not been seen entering.

Virginia City was whooping it up, like all the other towns in Alder Gulch. Sanders shut the door and locked it, turning to frown at his visitor.

"What are you doing here, Pryor? Sheriff Plummer has warrants out for you and a shoot-on-sight order. His deputies or any-one else could drill you without a challenge. He's fussed and fumed at us because we ran you away from the lynch mob. Williams and I have had to lie low and keep mighty quiet."

"No time to talk things over, Colonel," the Rio Kid said hurriedly. "As for Plummer, put this in yore pipe and smoke it! He's Chief of the Innocents, and Helm's his right-hand man!"

"What! You must be off your head, Captain!"

Wilbur Sanders jumped violently. He stared deep into the reckless, but honest eyes of the Rio Kid.

"There ain't the faintest doubt of it," Pryor insisted. "He's been tippin' the gang off to gold shipments and other information they could use in their work. And him bein' what he is prevents any real law work from goin' on against 'em. Think it over when yuh have time and yuh'll see how it all fits together, like a cut-up puzzle yuh work out. Plummer's after that million in gold yuh mean to start out Saturday night. He'll furnish twenty guards for yuh who'll stop any resistance the rest of yore men may make."

Sanders turned white under his brown whiskers. He licked his lips nervously.

"You — you know everything! Now I believe you, for Plummer did offer us a score of guards. The moving of the bullion is supposed to be a secret. Only Williams, Plummer and I knew of it, and I'll swear to Jim keeping quiet about it as I would to myself."

"Hurry!" said Pryor, turning. "Dig up as many fighters as yuh can and follow me to

142

Jefferson, Colonel. Boone Helm and a big gang are attackin' the settlers there tonight. I'm startin' on ahead."

"I'll do what I can," Sanders promised. "But it's hard to get men to fight the Innocents. I'll be along, if I have to come alone."

The Rio Kid shook the colonel's hand and hurried out. Springing to the dun's back, he sped from the town and up the Gulch road, straight for Jefferson.

It was near midnight when he heard guns, and knew that the attack had begun.

He took the bypath to the little settlement, up on the rocky hillside over the creek. Guns suddenly blazed at him, and he felt the *whoosh* of leaden slugs close to him as he whipped his Colt and fired at the flashes. A curse shrilled in the frosty air as the dun fled on.

Bedlam sounds came from the settlement. The Innocents were there, as thick as ants, it seemed. Heavy guns roared, and the speeding Rio Kid could see masses of killers silhouetted against the snow. Strange red glows showed in the windows of several of the wickiups and cabins that Roberts and his friends had built. The Rio Kid opened up as he raced by masked horsemen. They replied, and he sought a spot from which to fight, unable to get in closer, for they were too many for him.

Guns were bleating from narrow windows as the miners tried to fight back.

"Now what are they up to!" muttered the Rio Kid, as he saw an Innocent who had crept up under a dark cabin wall throw something through a window and turn to run.

A moment later the interior of the building showed red.

"The devils are throwin' powder smoke-pots!" he shouted into the wind.

The door of Taze Roberts' little shack burst open. Evidently the strangling vapor from a smokepot tossed in had been too much for young Roberts who appeared in the opening, framed against the light. Behind him showed the white face of his young wife, Elizabeth. With a howl of fury, the Innocents peppered the doorway with lead. Taze Roberts went down, gun in hand, his wife falling dead on top of him.

The fiendish plan that Boone Helm and Henry Plummer had thought up, as a way to get their victims out in the open where they could be killed was working well. The exploding smokepots could not be picked up and hurled back, since they blew up as they hit, with short fuses sputtering.

In General Roberts' bigger cabin, the same ruby glow was showing in the windows. Adam Byrne was in there, and the old general, leader of the doughty pioneers, with his daughter.

Another door opened as the people who lived in a small wickiup were forced out, gasping for air, eyes blinded and watering from smoke.

"Andy Lee!" muttered the Rio Kid. Lee was a Virginian, and his wife and two children lived in the wickiup with him.

Looking upon the horrible massacre ordered by Henry Plummer and staged by the Innocents, crazed the Rio Kid beyond the point where he could hold himself in. With both guns gripped in his hands he roared a challenge and charged at the masked devils who were covering Lee's home.

Their guns were leaping to mow down anything that moved in the drifting smoke. Straight at them the Rio Kid tore, his pistols snapping. The heavy slugs ripped a gaping hole in one outlaw's side, and knocked another over. Three others, however, pulled the triggers of their shotguns, and Lee's wife screamed and went down on her knees, then keeled over on her side and lay quiet.

Lee, with insensate fury, charged the killers, ignoring the buckshot that had bitten his hide. He fired point-blank into a masked face, blowing the Innocent's head off. But others pushed pistols against his back and drove lead into him.

Children were wailing. The Rio Kid, shooting straight and true, downed two more of the murderers before they broke and ran around Lee's cabin, escaping from his vengeful guns.

Bullets were hunting him, shrieking thick as hail in the air. The frail wickiup wall took fire rapidly, for the brush wall was dry from the heat inside, and blazed up, its red glow illuminating the clearing. It showed the zigzagging, raging Rio Kid, still in the Confederate gray, his eyes flaming his hate. His Colts were taking toll every time they spoke.

"Kill that man!" shouted Boone Helm. This man must not be allowed to interfere with the ghastly operations. The Innocents knew they must wipe out Jefferson, to protect themselves. These people could identify them as murderers and thieves. General Roberts, in fact, had already made a direct complaint against Boone Helm and other Innocents to Sheriff Plummer.

Swerving left, as Helm and his gunmen sent a whooshing volley his way, one that cut the night air a yard from him, the Rio

Kid drove to attack the bandit crew surrounding General Roberts' cabin. Guns
blazed from the windows as the defenders
sought to hurl back the enemy. But their
heads were visible as they shot, against the
light made by exploding smoke-bombs that
had been tossed in, and before they could
all be thrown back out, the damage was
done.

Three masked figures were on the side
of the cabin the Rio Kid whirled up to.
He tore one to pieces with the last bullets
in one gun and, drawing a spare Colt,
dusted the other two around the turn with
lead.

Rasping coughs could be heard in Roberts' home. The glass in the windows had
been smashed by bullets, and the Rio Kid
glimpsed the leonine head of the Confederate brigadier, a horse pistol in one hand, as
Roberts jumped to the window. Brave as
the lion he resembled Roberts was determined to fight to the death.

"It's Pryor, Roberts — don't shoot," bellowed the Rio Kid, his voice carrying over
the roar of the guns. "Help's comin'! Hold
out!"

"We can't" — Roberts broke off, gagging
and coughing — "stay in here much longer
— Cap'n — smoke too thick." He wheezed

but managed to yell, "Look out, behind you!"

The Rio Kid whipped around in his leather, his Colt cutting splinters from the wooden corner of the cabin as several dark figures stole around to take him. His quick action startled them, and their gunshots went wild over him.

There was no sense or use in his entering the cabin. He could do more good outside. Rage blazed within him at the thought of how well the horrible plan of Boone Helm and Plummer was working. Within a short time the folks of Jefferson would be smoked out of their homes like gophers from a hole in the ground. Smoked out, with eyes half-blinded, and lungs heaving from acrid vapor, unable to fight. Then Helm and his overpowering gang could kill them at leisure.

The dun jumped and swore in horse language, baring his long yellow teeth as a bullet burnt his tough gray hide.

"Move!" yelped the Rio Kid, touching him with his knee. "This is worse than Gettysburg!"

A compact body of Innocents, flashing from the ghostly, leafless trees, charged in upon him. Their fire drove him away from the Roberts' cabin as he snarled back at

148

them with his Colts.

He needed a moment in which to reload his guns, for his hidden spare pair had also been emptied. They were the new-fangled Colts, the most modern design, and their metallic cartridges were easier to carry and load than the nipple and cap more usually in use. It was to his advantage that the outlaws could not fire with the facility that he could.

With fingers that trembled with eagerness to get at the foe once more, the Rio Kid hastily reloaded his hot guns.

Chapter XV
Aftermath
of Massacre

With icy dread in his heart, the Rio Kid realized that within minutes the settlers would be forced outside, to die on the guns of the Innocents. They would have but a short time to live.

He cut past a wickiup, its windows glowing with the fire inside, which the dwellers were trying to beat out. Coughs came from the wickiup, as they had from the Roberts' home.

"Hold out!" he bellowed again. "Help's comin'!"

They *must* hold out, for once in the open the outlaws could murder them at will!

Helm, with bitter vengeance in his murderous soul, was after the Rio Kid, with a big bunch of masked devils raving for his blood. Bob Pryor might have ridden off, might have saved himself, but that was not his way. He preferred to fight it out, helping his friends, and he deliberately cut off his own chance of life by leaping from Saber's back.

"Run, Saber!" he shouted. "Keep on out of it!"

He slapped the dun's flank, driving his equine comrade from the dangerous hail of bullets. A horse was too easy a target and there was no sense in having Saber killed.

As he dived behind some boulders Helm and his men roared in triumph, believing they had him. From his higher point he could command most of the clearing and see the dark figures of the Innocents waiting for the kill. Jefferson was still bravely fighting, but the break was due to come any minute, for humans could not live in that deadly smoke.

The rocks gave Pryor protection, and he had craftily picked a spot which the enemy could not approach from the rear, for they would be blocked by thick-boled oaks growing in a clump. With his last shot he knocked an Innocent from his horse, and as the rest slowed, unwilling to attack head-on against the Rio Kid's shooting, and with him shielded, he rapidly shoved fresh shells into his pistols. He got two of them loaded before they sensed why he was not shooting, and Helm sang out orders for a charge.

He met them with bitter lead that stung

with death. As long as he could, he held them there, but they could not stomach his fire and turned their mustangs, taking shelter at a safer distance.

"We'll get that skunk later!" he heard Helm yell, and the tall, sneering-faced devil went back to finish the slaughter of Jefferson.

With his guns blazing, the Rio Kid sought to stem the irresistible tide that threatened to engulf all in the little settlement. Doors were being thrown open, for the occupants of the cabins were unable to stand the smoke any longer. The glows inside several cabins meant that the walls were afire.

Agony in his heart, the Rio Kid fought on, aware that death was close.

Then it came — that moment the Rio Kid had so dreaded. The utmost limit of human endurance had been reached, and he heard Boone Helm's shriek of ghastly triumph as people began staggering from cabins and wickiups, leaving their protective walls, falling face down in frozen mud and snow patches as they gasped for fresh air.

"Kill!" roared Helm. "Kill them all!"

Cursing, the Rio Kid, guns in both hands, leaped up and raced down the hill, shooting, oblivious to the bullets shrieking about his head, sent by the Innocents left to guard his rock nest.

Roberts' door had opened, and the old general emerged, with Adam Byrne at his side. They had their arms around Dorothy, trying to shield her from bullets.

The Rio Kid dashed on, blasting at the Innocents, who were on the point of massacring the entire population of Jefferson.

It was with the greatest astonishment of his life that he found them backing away from his guns. In his ears the crash of gunfire was deafening, as his heady Colts roared, smashing in his pounding drums.

Boone Helm was first to turn, the gangling, fiery-eyed leader of the Innocents leading the way off the field of battle. Masked devils followed in bunches, spurring their animals up the rough slope for the ridge, their rowels digging in until blood spurted as they beat their mounts on with pistol barrels.

The astounded Pryor did not comprehend what had caused this retreat. It seemed a miracle.

But as the fire of the outlaws slackened, he heard slugs whipping the air over his head.

Then he saw that from the gulch road riders were galloping quickly in on the settlement, shooting from the saddle.

There were about a dozen of them — led by Colonel Wilbur Sanders and Captain James Williams.

"At them, boys!" shouted the burly Williams. "Fetch up the rest — pronto!"

The Innocents at the ridge looked back. The fearless Vigilantes under Williams and Sanders charged up the slope, shooting. They passed through the lane of smoking cabins, furiously anxious to come to grips with the enemy, although they were outnumbered.

The Rio Kid sank to one knee in the snow. The effect of his wound, the terrific strain of the battle, which he had saved by his delaying action, holding Helm and his gang until Sanders could come up, had hit him now that help had arrived.

Faint cheers rose from the throats of Roberts' friends, as they realized that the massacre had been checked.

Sanders, Williams, Bielder and the trusted vigilantes with them, fresh and ready to fight to the death with the bandits, were on the ridge now. The Innocents, realizing they could not finish off the helpless people of Jefferson, were in full retreat, scattering, shooting back, wildly fleeing.

Adam Byrne hurried to his friend's side.

"Bob, are you hurt?" he choked.

"No — no. Done in, that's all — blast the devils!"

His eyes burned and faintness all but overcame him as Byrne helped him to his feet, and they walked slowly to the Roberts' cabin. The general had seized a pail and was throwing water from a filled tub on the licking blaze inside.

"Form bucket lines to the creek!" Roberts shouted. "We've got to save the buildings!"

As some formed a bucket brigade, other sad-faced pioneers began picking up the wounded, carrying them inside Roberts' cabin in which the fire had been extinguished, and the smoke fanned out. A wound might prove fatal if the victim were not kept warm and cared for.

Lamps were lighted, and candles, as the devastated people took stock. Dorothy Roberts, her eyes wide with shock from what she had looked upon that night, was helping with the injured. A cloth was bound around her left forearm, and fresh blood showed on it. A slug had nicked her soft flesh.

When the Rio Kid found the girl had been wounded, and already knowing that Taze Roberts' wife had died with her husband, as another woman had also died, he could scarcely contain his fury.

"I'll take them!" he cried. "Every man jack! Women-killers! If lead don't do it, they'll stretch hemp!"

"Sit down and take it easy," ordered the grim-lipped Adam Byrne. "There is nothin' to do right now, Bob."

So great was his relief that Dorothy had been spared, and that the main body of people had been saved, that it was difficult for young Byrne to speak. But he knew that Bob Pryor needed water, food, rest.

Byrne brought a tall glass of whiskey to the Rio Kid who was sitting on a bench with his head in his hands. Pryor downed it. Roberts, too, had a drink. The general was scratched and shaken but had received no serious hurts.

As the settlers brought in their wounded for treatment, the sobbing of the bereaved began. Fires were doused, the bucket brigade from the creek doing the trick as the shooting above grew more distant.

"You held 'em, Captain," Roberts growled, pausing a moment by the Rio Kid. "They would have had us all if you hadn't delayed them."

The Rio Kid shook his head sadly. "They got plenty, General. But they'll pay for it."

"Let's hope so. This country ain't fit for decent folks to live in."

Roberts' Southern chivalry was outraged by the attack upon women and children. He could not comprehend bestiality that permitted such horror.

Two hours later Sanders, Williams and Biedler, and their friends returned.

Several carried creases from bullets, but they had driven the Innocents into the wilds of the mountains.

Sanders dismounted, his lieutenants following suit. Their faces were streaked with powder smoke, and bleeding from scratches where whiplike branches had cut.

"We didn't have enough men to take them and wipe them out," Sanders growled. "These were all I was able to rout out, Pryor. There are too many men around here who don't care, or who are afraid of the Innocents."

When the cold gray of dawn broke upon the scene it showed wickiups blackened ruins, but the rest of the settlement had been saved. Under blankets lay the dead, while Roberts' home, warmed by a roaring pine-log blaze, was filled to overflowing with women and children, with wounded, and with those who had lost their shacks.

Sanders and his men were camped in the square, on guard. Hot coffee and food had been served. The Rio Kid had slept the sleep of sheer exhaustion, and now he began to spruce up. He shaved off the beard stubble and combed his hair, washed the grime and blood from his flesh, and donned his own dry clothing which he had left at the Roberts'.

He was pale under his tan, but his shoulders were squared. He sought out Sanders, whose grave face was sad.

"Send some of yore men through Alder Gulch, Colonel," he suggested, "and tell folks to come here and take a look."

Sanders stared at him. "All right. We've nothing to lose."

By the time the sun was up, the fruits of the Rio Kid's idea became tangible. Messengers had filtered swiftly through the Gulch towns, and men and even some women were arriving at Jefferson to see the sights after the horrible attack.

Under a long shed lay the stiffened dead. Miners, rough, stalwart, most of them honest fellows and decent at heart, filed past the pitiful victims. They removed their flat-brimmed hats and caps, awkward in their movements from embarrassment and pity for those who had so suffered.

The Rio Kid stood near at hand, watching with Colonel Sanders. Men would come up, look at the dead. Then they would start as they saw the murdered women. Profanity exploded from bearded lips.

"Look — they kilt women! Women!"

They passed on but they did not leave the settlement, gathering in hoarsely whispering knots, heads together.

"I think it's working," grunted Colonel Sanders.

Eyes went steely, or flashed with sudden fury as they fixed upon the victims of the Innocents. More and more miners crowded into Jefferson. A buzz of threatening anger, the rage of the righteous against the evil, grew in volume.

CHAPTER XVI
THE VIGILANTES

Low-voiced orders were given by Sanders to his trusted dozen. Williams, Biedler, and other lieutenants began sifting through the crowd, whispering in the ears of men known to be decent and above-board. Usually the man so addressed would nod, gladly. What the citizens of Alder Gulch had looked upon that morning was enough to sweep aside all doubts, all fear.

"Why, nobody's safe!" the Rio Kid heard a burly miner growl. "Not even kids and women. Somethin's got to be done and pronto."

"Yuh're right, Dan," another agreed, and there was a murmur of accord.

"Say, Sanders, I'm sorry I didn't ride with yuh last night," said a big fellow with a red beard. "I wasn't aimin' to horn in on what seemed none of my business. But now I savvy it is, and I'm goin' to make it so. I'm with yuh on anything."

"Good man, Carstairs."

Sanders stepped closer, whispered in Carstairs' hairy ear, and the miner nodded, with a grin.

"I'll be there," he promised.

A horseman, riding alone, appeared from the Gulch road. The Rio Kid, glancing at him, recognized Henry Plummer, sheriff of Bannack and Virginia City. Pryor's face was a mask as he watched the murderous, thieving hypocrite. But he was thinking, "You shore will stretch hemp, hombre!"

Plummer rode up and dismounted. He was always the gentleman, his voice quiet and cool. He glanced at Sanders, at Pryor, and at General Roberts.

"This is a terrible thing," he said, sadly, shaking his head. "Word just reached me of it, friends. I swear I will do everything within my power as sheriff to bring the murderers to justice."

"That's the way to talk, Plummer," Sanders said heartily, slapping him on the back.

Many of the people greeted the sheriff, unaware of his perfidy. Only those trusted men, checked by and known to Sanders, Williams and Biedler were let in on the terrible secret which the Rio Kid had discovered.

A guard was left at Jefferson and the worn,

shattered inhabitants rested, sleeping through the day. The Rio Kid, frazzled by what he had undergone, stole a long nap in the afternoon, but before dark he saddled Saber who was all right except for scratches he had picked up when he had run off, and took the road to Virginia City.

It was Friday. On the morrow the huge gold shipment was to be sent out to the Government mint. On the outskirts of the settlement stood the big warehouse in which the Rio Kid knew the bullion was being held under guard. It was dark, apparently, at first sight. But silent figures wearing pistol belts and carrying rifles or shotguns, according to the user's preference, stood in the shadows.

John X. Biedler came out to intercept the Rio Kid as he pulled the dun off the road to the warehouse. He seized the dun's bridle, looking up at Pryor.

"Oh — howdy, Cap'n. Sanders and Williams are inside."

Dismounting, the Rio Kid passed the gauntlet of armed guards and was admitted through a side door. A short corridor led him into an unheated, high-ceilinged room at the rear of the storehouse. It had a dirt floor, and wooden walls. The three windows had been carefully covered with black cloth to shut off leakage of light to the outside. Boxes, benches, logs of wood made improvised seats.

About seventy miners and other citizens of the Gulch and surrounding country had already come in. Up front, at a flat-topped, unpainted slab table on which were paper, a bottle of ink and pens, sat Colonel Wilbur Sanders and his right-hand man, Captain James Williams.

Sanders nodded and signaled the Rio Kid to come over.

"Sit down beside me," he ordered.

More men were passed through. Every one was a trusted citizen, picked by the first dozen men under Sanders. High Sheriff Henry Plummer was conspicuous by his absence.

When the doors were locked, and guarded by Biedler and another miner with shotguns across their arms, about a hundred men were in the room.

"Gentlemen," said Wilbur Sanders in his deep, stirring voice, "the meeting of the Montana Vigilantes will now come to order."

He paused for a pregnant moment, looking over the assemblage, then went on:

"Hardly a day passes that a murder or robbery isn't committed hereabouts. The toughs have had it their own way for a long time. No man who hits it rich or wins at cards, no bullion shipment or stage, can hope to escape them except by luck. Spies keep a sharp eye out for anything of value so the road-agents can take it. Anyone who dares complain is waylaid and murdered.

"I'm saying what all of you already know. We have all been preoccupied with our hunt for the earth's treasures and no one has wanted to be bothered about civil affairs. What happened to the other fellow, the victim of the Innocents, has not appeared to count with us. But from this moment on it is to be different. Alder Gulch is growing up. Every man here is a picked and trusted person, and sworn to secrecy."

The Rio Kid listened as Wilbur Sanders rapidly formulated the constitution of the Montana Vigilantes. When they had been written out the start of the momentous document read:

REGULATIONS AND BY-LAWS
This Committee shall consist of a President or chief, and Executive Officer, Secretary, Treasurer, Executive Committee, Captains and Lieutenants of Companies.

The rules that followed were read to the

quietly listening men. Wilbur Sanders was chief, and Jim Williams executive officer, charged with seeing to it that the Vigilante orders were carried out. The executive committee consisted of seventeen carefully chosen men from different towns, and it was their duty to make certain that sentences were immediately carried out, the only punishment to be inflicted being death.

Members were required to report to the committee any criminal acts that came to their knowledge. A solemn oath of secrecy was administered to every Vigilante. Sanders warned that not even the sheriff or other law officers were to be informed of their plans.

"So far," said Sanders, "we have been able to identify only a handful of the Innocents positively, and we are not going to hang a man on hearsay and gossip, gentlemen. But now that our organization is complete, we expect to begin picking up those we know for certain have killed victims on the road."

"Could I say a word, Colonel?" asked the Rio Kid.

"Yes, most surely. Vigilantes, this is Captain Robert Pryor, who may be trusted to the hilt. He has already given us most vital and valuable information. Forget any charges made by Plummer or others against him. They are entirely false."

"Thanks," drawled Pryor. "My idea's this. Instead of pickin' up what few outlaws we savvy and scarin' the rest into the hills where we can't take 'em, let's wait a couple days till I see if I can obtain a complete list of the gang."

"But where could yuh hope to find such a list?" asked Captain Jim Williams, eagerly but doubtful. "Those devils don't go round signin' their names to papers."

"I wouldn't shoot off my mouth if I didn't have a good idea, gents," the Rio Kid said apologetically. "Now, has any man in the audience ever heard of a tall hombre in these parts callin' hisself George Carter? He wears gambler clothes and has dark curly hair."

No one had. Blank looks were exchanged and the Rio Kid decided that he must hunt out the Confederate spy himself.

All had solemnly taken the Vigilante oath, and plans were laid for the organization, which was to endure for years, a bulwark against lawlessness in the new Montana that was to be. The Montana Vigilantes never hung a man who did not deserve it, and none ever exposed his friends.

A detail of armed men was designated to stand guard over Jefferson until the Innocents were broken, so there could be no repetition of the horrible massacre.

Jim Williams, John X. Biedler and the other members of the Executive Committee, including Pryor, stayed behind as the main session broke up. For the Rio Kid was to act in the capacity of a confidential adviser to Wilbur Sanders, President, and brains of the Vigilantes.

It was half-past eleven when Pryor and Sanders finished their plans for the gold shipment.

"Boone Helm's meetin' Plummer around midnight," the Rio Kid reminded. "We'd better get started, Colonel."

"All right. Come along, Williams, we'll go up to the sheriff's office now. You know the way, don't you, Pryor?"

"Shore. I was in there, remember?"

He slipped off into the shadows, taking to the back alleys. Williams and Sanders walked up the main street to the sheriff's office, in which a light was burning up front.

Plummer let them in, nodding in a quiet, friendly fashion.

"Good evening, Sheriff," said Sanders pleasantly, as Plummer invited them inside. "You're on duty late."

"Lots of business pressing, Sanders. Sit down."

"Thanks. We've been perfecting our plans for the big gold shipment tomorrow evening. We mean to start after dark. You'll furnish us with additional guards as you promised?"

"Oh, certainly, with pleasure, Sanders," Plummer said heartily. "I've got twenty picked men for you, and you can have more if you want 'em."

Colonel Sanders nodded thoughtfully.

"That should be sufficient," he said, "since we've kept our plans secret. No one will even guess we've got such a valuable cargo. It's to look like a food-supply train, but once we get to the other end of the Gulch, we'll strike fast for the Salt Lake City Trail."

"It sounds all right," agreed Plummer. And he asked casually, "Of course you'll use the Pioneer Cutoff, Sanders? It's fifteen miles shorter."

"Oh, yes," Sanders said innocently. "And we'll have the same number of armed guards you are furnishing."

"Are you goin' along, Sanders?" asked Plummer.

Sanders shook his head. "Not this time, but I reckon on sending Williams as captain of the guards."

Jim Williams cleared his throat.

"I'm dry as old boot leather. I'll get me a drink from in back, Henry."

"Help yourself," said Plummer. "The bucket's standin' on the bench by the bull-pen."

CHAPTER XVII
PLOT AND
COUNTERPLOT

Jim Williams strolled through into the rear of the jail, while Sanders continued his talk with Plummer.

"You'll be on hand for the start, won't you, Sheriff?" he asked rather loudly, in his clear, fine voice. "Better bring your detail of guards over yourself. I flatter myself we've kept this mighty quiet and it should go through without a hitch."

"We'll hope so," said the sheriff heartily. "But of course, with forty men ridin', you can never tell, Sanders. It's best to be on the safe side."

In the rear, out of sight of the sheriff's position, a tin dipper clattered against an iron bucket where Williams was getting a drink of water. Williams strolled back into the front office, and sat down. Plummer offered West Indian cheroots, which the two visitors lighted up. Then they shook hands with the lawman and left.

"I'm worn out, and I'm hitting for bed right away, Jim," Sanders said to Williams, standing in the door.

The mild-eyed, gentlemanly sheriff shut and softly slid the bolt of the door. From a window he watched the two who had just left him pause at the corner, and split up, each going to his home.

By the clock on Plummer's desk it was two minutes before midnight.

With his catlike tread he walked into the big rear chamber, with the bull-pen and the cells behind it on his left. A small storeroom, with its door closed, and a square closet filled with brooms, mops, pails and other necessary impedimenta, including spare saddles and equipment with which to fit out posses was to the right. The back was dark save for the streak of light coming from the open passage.

The gray smoke of the sheriff's cheroot twined lazily about his head. His right arm, crippled in a shooting affray some time before, rested in a constrained position on his holstered six-shooter. Inside his ruffled coat was his real killer, a slim-barreled .38 of modern design. After his right hand had been made almost useless because of his wound, he had practiced assiduously with his left until it and his left eye had become

171

as proficient in drawing speed and accuracy as his right had been. That was his business, and few men could beat Henry Plummer to the shot.

He paced up and down, blowing out puffs of smoke, restless as a caged tiger. When the clock struck twelve he went to the alley door and put his ear to it. Soon he heard stealthy footsteps, then a soft scratching on the wooden panel.

"I am innocent!" a hoarse whisper gave the password of the gang.

"I am innocent!" Plummer replied, and slid back the heavy iron bolt.

Boone Helm quickly came in. A dirty bandage was on his whiskered cheek. The sheriff closed the door and shot the bolt.

"Is it all right?" asked Helm in a whisper. "I seen Sanders go into his house as I came in."

"He was here," growled Plummer. "Williams too." He spoke in normal tones, and Helm realized that they were alone. "We'll stay back here, though, out of the light. Anybody's apt to come to the office at any time of day or night. That was a bad job you boys did at Jefferson. The whole Gulch is roused up over it, and you failed to kill the very men I wanted put out of the way."

Helm cursed. "Thank that Rio Kid devil

for it, Henry. He held us up till Sanders got there. Cut us up bad, too."

"I don't like the smell of things, in general," Plummer growled, chewing on his cheroot.

"Why? What in all tarnation can they do?" Plummer shook his head, unconvinced.

"Sanders was almost too smooth and pleasant tonight," Plummer said ruminatively. "I may get out after this job, Boone, but keep that to yourself. You know, I was in California and in Oro Fino in Idaho. I savvy when a man's reached the end of the rope."

"Aw, it's nothin' but big-mouth talk," snarled Helm contemptuously. "We're too strong for 'em, Henry. Remember when they tried to string up Lyons and Buck? Huh, that was a joke! The women cried 'em out of the noose."

"Hmm, that's true. Just the same, I'm thinkin' about hitting the road for good after this. . . . Now as to details. It's as I told you — a million in gold, packed on mules, and guarded by forty men. I'm furnishin' twenty, and they'll work with you when the time comes. Hit at dawn at the south end of Pioneer Cutoff. There's plenty of rocks up above and the trail there is as narrow as a weasel's eyes. You lost a bunch of men, killed or wounded at Jefferson. How many have you got comin'?"

"About seventy. I've called in our road-agents and tippers from every town in the Gulch and as far as Bannack. The twenty you send with the train'll make it a dead cinch. We'll shoot down the whole passel of 'em."

"Williams will be in that guard," reminded Plummer. "Make sure you kill him first of all. And Carter likewise. As soon as you've done them in, drive the gold train on the trail south, as though you meant to make for Salt Lake City. Then we'll switch the loads to horses and cover their tracks. I'll meet you beyond the Cutoff with fresh pack animals, and some of the boys can drive the mules on to lead off any pursuit. There oughtn't to be any trouble, though, not if it's pulled off carefully. Let none ride from that Cutoff alive, savvy? That will give us days in which to get clear."

"It's the biggest one yet, Chief;" chortled Boone Helm, rubbing his blood-stained, calloused hands.

More details were gone into, then Helm left the way he had come, and Henry Plummer locked the back door which gave into the black recesses of Tin Can Alley. Up the way, people in saloons and honky-tonks were raising hob. They would keep it up until dawn, making the Gulch howl, while respectable citizens, with their homes darkened, slumbered.

Henry Plummer stood listening to the receding steps of Helm. He looked about the dim-lit room and at the cells in which there were no prisoners. When he moved, his footfalls echoed hollowly as if the very plastered walls were aware that horrible secrets, of murder and perfidy and every sort of crime were locked in this man's black heart.

He was a whited sepulchre. Most inhabitants of Alder Gulch, Bannack and Virginia City, while aware that he was a fast shot and had killed men in fights, did not believe him to be any worse than many who had come West to turn over a new leaf. He was the Law, quiet, admired by ladies to whom he was as polite as any cavalier.

He stood in the middle of the room for moments, frowning in deep thought.

"Yes," he muttered, "and if I must, I'll get out. I didn't like the way Sanders looked at me. The devil with the rest of them, Helm included. If he's fool enough to stay, that's his hard luck. But first I'll get that million."

He went up front, and blew out the lamp. In the darkness knowing the familiar office blindly, he took his hat and bearskin coat and went out, locking up after him, and heading over to the Bearcat for a nightcap. He was a moderate drinker and was seldom seen under the influence, another recommendation to the ladies of Alder Gulch, but he felt in the need of a drink now.

He was sitting at a table in the saloon, when the door of the store closet back at the jail opened, and a stealthy, dark figure emerged.

The Rio Kid, gun in hand, flitted to the corridor, made certain the jail was deserted, after hearing Plummer leave, then tiptoed to the back door, softly unbolted it, and looked up and down before he stepped outside.

"He'll figger he forgot to bolt her after Helm," he thought, as he closed the back door and melted into the shadows.

Bob Pryor had heard Plummer's secret plans. When Sanders had raised his voice, while they had been talking to Plummer earlier, Williams, in the back room, supposedly to get a drink of water, had unlocked the alley entrance and the Rio Kid had slipped in and hidden himself in the closet.

There was time for but little sleep for the Rio Kid, but he caught a necessary cat nap. Before dawn he was awake and had made his way to the warehouse where the gold was stored.

And it was not long before Bob Pryor and Captain Jim Williams were hidden in the dark room in which the Vigilantes had met, checking up on the start of the pack-train. The bold spying of the Rio Kid had apprized the men in charge of the gold of the Innocents' plans, and the Vigilantes had been able to lay their own counterplot.

Hearing voices outside, the Rio Kid slipped aside to look into the main storehouse.

"Good gravy!" he exclaimed, clutching at Jim Williams' brawny arm for Williams had followed him, "there's the man I'm after!"

"Ssh — they might hear yuh!" whispered Williams. "Who? Which one?"

"See the feller in Union blue, wearin' a major's uniform? He's talkin' to Sanders now!"

Williams peeked through the narrow crack into the main storehouse, where stood lines of bridled mules, with roped wooden boxes balanced on either side of their tawny bodies.

"Why, Pryor, that's Major Smythe, Pryor!" said Williams.

"Smythe? Smythe, my eye! That's George Carter, the —"

He broke off. He had taken Sanders and Williams into his confidence to some extent, but not entirely. They did not know that President Lincoln had sent the Rio Kid to Montana, that he was in reality on special Intelligence duty for the United States.

"Aw no," Jim Williams insisted. "Smythe has been here for near a year, Cap'n. He's a good friend of Sanders'. Mebbe I shouldn't say this, 'cause Smythe asked us not to tell, but he's on a secret mission from Washington. He's a bullion checker, here to see that the Johnny Rebs don't git any of this gold."

"Well, dang my perforated hide!" growled the Rio Kid. "He's clever, I got to admit that."

Flickering lanterns were suspended from the warehouse ceiling beams, giving light for the work. Wilbur Sanders took the lid off a box not yet nailed up, and exposed it for a moment. Men's eyes, including those of Henry Plummer, who was on hand to supply his promised guard detail, were greedily riveted on the fat yellow sheen of the gold.

Then Sanders shut the box and a helper nailed the top down. It was tied in a diamond hitch on one side of a mule, balancing a second of the same weight on the other.

"I'll ride along with the train for a few miles, Colonel, if that is satisfactory," the Rio Kid heard Carter, alias Major Smythe, say.

He now was an entirely different man from the dark-coated gambler for whom the Rio Kid had been hunting. In his trim blue uniform, with sword belt and Army pistol in black holster, the felt hat strapped low over his deep-set eyes, holding in his prominent ears, the Confederate spy played his part like the genius he was at such work.

"He shore knows his business," the Rio Kid thought admiringly. "He had me fooled!"

He realized that Carter had to work with what material he could find in the wild districts. He was ruthless in the way he was shuttling gold off to the Confederacy, shutting his eyes to the killings done by Boone Helm and his bunch.

"He has to trust Helm but he don't go any farther than he must," ruminated Pryor, as he figured on how to handle Carter. "Wonder what he'd do if he savvied that Helm and Plummer mean to double cross him?"

There was nothing Carter could do, he figured, except take such chances as were forced upon him. The spy was playing a dangerous game, and had to take things as they came.

The Rio Kid hoped to catch Carter and obtain the complete list of the Innocents which the man claimed to have in his possession. But, failing in this, Sanders and he planned to shoot down or capture as many bandits as possible in the attack on the train, then try to talk prisoners into exposing other Innocents.

"If I go after Carter now, he'll smell a rat and so'll Helm," the Rio Kid mused. "I better let him ride awhile, till the right moment comes. Anyhow, when he sees what happens, it'll open his eyes."

Chapter XVIII
The Gold Train

Upwards of half an hour later the long pack-train filed out of Green's warehouse and forded the creek, hitting the road to the Cutoff. Armed men rode the flanks, the van and the rear. Duly the click of hoofs, the soft rustle of leather, a cough now and then or an animal's snort, disturbed the night.

The Rio Kid did not ride with the train, much as he wished to be in the danger spot, once the Cutoff was reached. Jim Williams, who knew all the plans of the Vigilantes, had charge of the long procession. It had been decided that Pryor must stay out of sight, so as not to rouse Plummer's or Helm's suspicions before the battle opened.

Once the pack-train was on its way, the Rio Kid, on Saber, joined Colonel Sanders, Chief of the Vigilantes. They started swiftly for the rough ridge trails, leaving Virginia City in a different direction than that taken by the pack-train.

Two miles outside of town, they were hailed by men waiting in a big mountain meadow, armed men with faces grim in the pale moonlight. Pistols and rifles sheened in the faint illumination reflected from the snow. Some sixty miners were there with fast mustangs. Vigilantes sworn to carry out to the death their leader's commands.

The false charges brought against Bob Pryor by Henry Plummer had been explained away by Colonel Sanders so now the Vigilantes knew the Rio Kid to be a trusted ally.

The Rio Kid, expert at scouting, took the lead, with Sanders riding at his side. Companies of Vigilantes fell into semi-military formation, led by captains and lieutenants designated by Sanders and Williams. At last the men of Alder Gulch had united against the criminals who had cowed them for so long.

Hardly a rider was in the crowd — miner, storekeeper, townsman — who had not seen the horrible work of the Innocents. They had seen dead bodies left for the wolves and vultures, beaten victims, people robbed of all for which they had toiled. Many Vigilantes had lost gold or friends and relatives to the road-agents, before this doing nothing, while Plummer and his gang made a mockery of justice.

They rode for three hours. Sanders knew the trails, and the Rio Kid watched for sign, stopping now and then to peer closely at what possibly were tracks, shading a lighted match in one hand for light. He did not wish to run upon any bands of outlaws heading for the Cutoff ambush.

About two A.M., the weather suddenly changed, as if by magic. The cold was swept away and a warm gush of air struck the men in the face. Cracklings that increased in volume, as though the world were splitting up, began all about them.

"What the —" the surprised Rio Kid exclaimed.

"It's the Chinook," Sanders informed him. "It'll melt the snow rapidly, Pryor. The ground may be clear by dawn."

It was Bob Pryor's first experience of the Chinook, the wind from the mountains. Rushing so rapidly down the steep slopes that' it became heated from friction, the Chinook blew through the Northwest in the early spring, cleaning off the snow and ice from the lower reaches of the mountains.

In a short time, the going became slushy, then soggy as the frost began coming out of the ground.

"We're not making the time we should

reach the Cutoff, Pryor!" exclaimed Sanders.

Nature had played one of her strange pranks which made the best laid plans of mice and men go wrong despite every effort to prevent errors.

"It'll slow the train down, too," observed Pryor.

"Yes. But they're ahead of us, and they're on a well-beaten road — not a mountain trail. I'm afraid Helm has his gang in position by this time."

"But we've got to be there to help Williams when the outlaws strike," the Rio Kid said grimly. "Otherwise —"

There was no need to finish. Sanders knew as well as he that Captain Jim Williams and his score of daredevils who had volunteered for the dangerous job of sticking with the gold-train, must be quickly reinforced or they would be shot down by Plummer's overwhelming forces. Twenty of the sheriff's hired killers were riding with the gold-train, ready to shoot them in the backs.

The earth rapidly became soft mud, bursting up as the air puffed the sod, melted by the Chinook. The horses sank to the hocks in many spots, while rocks, freed from their winter's sockets, rolled under hoof. The splittings and cracklings sounded loud in the Rio Kid's anxious ears.

"How far now to the Cutoff, Sanders?" he asked for the twentieth time.

"About two hours, at this rate."

"Huh! And the dawn comes within sixty minutes, anyways! Listen, I'm goin' on! Saber can make a little better time than this."

"I'll go with you. This trail leads straight to the Cutoff."

"Pick the fastest hosses and foller me. Tell the others to come as fast as they're able."

At Sanders' commands, Vigilantes with powerful, swift steeds rode to form an advance squad, but by the time they had started, the Rio Kid had pushed down the slope and was riding up the next hill.

"We got to make it, Saber! We can't let 'em get away with it!"

He begged the dun for more speed, and Saber fought to respond. Balls of red mud flew from the animal's hoofs.

The winding way was easy enough to make out in the waning moonlight as it ran up and down, crossed razor-back ridges, gullies with streams beginning to rise from the melting snow, and through evergreen forests, gloomily dark and foreboding. The bare limbs of other trees were starkly outlined against the starry sky, and the Chinook blew so hot that the Rio Kid had to open his jacket.

Doggedly he pushed on as creamy lather broke out all over the dun. Saber was breathing hard as he took the long hills at his best lope.

Sanders and his men were coming on, but none of their mounts could match the dun's endurance and speed. Finally the Rio Kid was no longer able to see the others behind him. And a faint touch of gray told him that dawn was close at hand.

"On, Saber!" he muttered, loosening his pistols in their holsters. Under his leg rode his Army carbine, loaded and ready.

It was agony to think of Jim Williams and the intrepid score of fighting men, counting upon their friends to arrive in time to hit the gang, being disappointed. He could imagine their mounting uneasiness as the attack progressed and they were unrelieved.

Then in the east the Rio Kid saw a tiny bit of white, with a dull redness streaking the horizon. Sweat was pouring from him as, in the mounting light of the new day, he drove toward Pioneer Cutoff.

He nearly ran Saber over the edge of a steep cliff, a hundred-foot drop, but the sure-footed mustang checked, sliding to a halt.

At that instant gunshots suddenly roared, echoing in the black depths of the canyon into which he had almost plunged.

"This is it!" he muttered, hastily pulling his carbine from its sling.

Bedlam had broken loose in the narrow slit in the mountains, known as Pioneer Pass or Pioneer Cutoff. The light was rapidly growing as the Rio Kid hunted a way down. From what he had overheard at Plummer's office the previous night he knew that the bulk of the Innocents were lurking at a spot where the canyon narrowed down until a horse could almost leap it.

The shooting was not far away, and as he hit the rocks, and ran in its direction, he topped a shelf of reddish rock and could see into the depression. In the shadows still there, the long mule train had pulled to a halt. He recognized Jim Williams as the burly Vigilante fought like a cornered lion against Plummer's men.

The trap had been sprung a trifle too soon. The Rio Kid was to learn, later, that Williams had been unwilling to push his troop any farther into the Cutoff, since the Chinook had told him that Sanders and his men might be delayed.

The plan had been to allow the ambush to proceed, and draw in the main forces of the Innocents to a spot where they could be mowed down by Sanders' Vigilantes. The first great peril to the Williams men would be the traitorous fire of the guards supplied by the sheriff. Williams' task would be to bring his men out of the ambush alive, and when they retreated, the Innocents would pursue, then Sanders' men would close in.

Now the attack had begun, and the Chief of the Vigilantes and his forces were still far behind.

The Rio Kid found a slanting rock slide that seemed to lead into the ravine. He started down it afoot, his carbine clutched in one hand and braking himself with the other. A call came to him from the right, and he saw two men with masked faces rear from a rock nest.

"Hey — is that you, Boone?"

They were Innocents, who had begun firing down at Williams' men.

More of them were in niches in the ravine walls. The Rio Kid threw a quick shot at the two he saw. It knocked one fellow backward against his startled mate.

Now he could see the Cutoff proper, its floor paved with shale and broken rocks and bare alders sticking from patches of dirt. It

188

was about two hundred yards wide at this point, and Williams had his score of fighting men beyond the pack-train. The mules were beginning to churn uneasily as gunfire grew in volume and the cursing shouts of battle rattled in the pass.

On Pryor's side of the pass, as he crouched on a narrow ledge, with the bulging red strata protecting him on one side, were the traitors, the supposed aides supplied by Henry Plummer. Carter, the Confederate spy, in his blue uniform, was among them. They were firing at Williams.

Rapidly, the Rio Kid's expert battle eye took in the layout. Williams had evidently got the jump on the killers, for they seemed confused, although they were shooting rapidly at the slowly retreating Vigilantes in the Cutoff. Several guards were busy trying to keep the pack-train from bolting.

Bullets were whirling in the ravine, slapping the rock walls. Two horses fell, and then one of Williams' Vigilantes slumped in his leather, holding his right shoulder which a slug had smashed. Williams made a short charge. The cold fury of the fighting Vigilante leader drew the admiration of the Rio Kid. Williams' pistols blared, and a crooked guard threw up both hands, shrieked, and fell from his mustang.

As Bob Pryor shot into the Plummer gang, breaking them up, the firing from the niches in the walls increased. An ominous, heavy, drumming of hoofs shook the floor of the canyon and fifty masked Innocents, led by Boone Helm, flashed into view.

"Move that train on out, blast yuh!" Boone Helm's snarling voice shrieked through the echoing cut. "After them skunks! Kill every man jack of 'em!"

The Rio Kid fired at the swift-moving target the man made, and Helm's Stetson flew off his head. The bandit chief swerved, and the Rio Kid's bullet missed him, but cut the nose off a bandit coming in Helm's wake. Spurting blood showed in the patterned beard as the outlaw whipped off his mask. He forgot all about the fight, screaming as he put both hands to his ruined nose.

More and more Innocents appeared, spurring in with deadly fury, guns raging at the retreating Williams and his men.

The battle was already raging, although Helm still had the majority of his killers set at the narrowest point of the Cutoff, to the south.

CHAPTER XIX
THE VIGILANTES RIDE

George Carter was most interested in the vast gold store in that mule-train. He was bawling orders, helping to get the mules going, to head them out of the Cutoff, to safety. Boone Helm, too, intrigued by that great mass of precious metal, was willing to go to any lengths to obtain it.

The Rio Kid's fire was hardly noticed by the big gang of Innocents with the pack-train. Their own friends were shooting into the ravine, and the first hits made by Pryor were thought to be from Williams' guns. But when he fired twice again, killing one bandit, and downing the horse of another, they came to life.

"Hey — look out up there!" roared an outlaw who had noted the spurts of flame and smoke from Pryor's carbine, and the angle at which it was pointed.

Helm veered over toward the mule-train. With three men with him, he bore down

191

upon George Carter, who was mounted on a big black stallion.

"They're goin' to kill Carter!" muttered Pryor, sweeping his carbine toward them.

Carter suddenly swung in his leather. He must have read his fate in the burning eyes of Boone Helm, for he jerked his reins suddenly, his big black rearing on its hind legs. The beast received Helm's first shot in the breast, and the others were balked for a moment by the bulk of the animal.

The Rio Kid was shooting. Helm cursed, putting his head down, hugging close to his mount. Pryor killed an outlaw who was coming around to take Carter in the rear as the Confederate's magnificent stallion hit the dirt, legs spreading.

Shooting as fast as he could, the Rio Kid downed a third in Helm's group. Boone Helm himself was backing off. Pryor got a fourth crooked guard as the mules were thrown forward. Then galloped on out of the Cutoff, disappearing into the narrows.

But the sheer mass of the attacking bandits was beating Williams and his men back.

"Why don't Sanders come!" muttered the Rio Kid.

A bullet cut through his Stetson, and he caught the flash of the pistol as a high-grader who had worked to a ledge above him tried for him. He could see the man's glittering eyes, the masked face and the flat black hat, the gun arm and hunched shoulder. He let go a snapshot, and the fellow jumped and hung with his head lolling over the rock edge.

"It's that Rio Kid down there!" a hoarse voice howled.

Men who had seen him descend to his vantage point above the ambush, and who knew him now, were closing in, seeking to finish him off.

He scrunched back against the steep red wall as far as he could, dropping his rifle and substituting a Colt. The train was gone from the Cutoff, and Boone Helm was taking aim at George Carter, who lay upon the ground on his face. Evidently Helm had made a hit while Pryor had been occupied with those killers trying for him from the rear.

The Rio Kid's Colt barked. Helm jumped, as his Navy revolver belched death lead. He suddenly leaped off his horse, and landed running. He was wounded but not seriously. He rushed across the flat, dodging his surging men, and leaped to the back of a horse from which the rider had been shot.

Bullets were cutting fragments that rained upon Pryor's head and body. The outlaws were working to ledges from which they could kill him. Still he fought on, trying to keep the killers from the senseless George Carter Williams and his men were fighting.

Boone Helm followed the gold. He did not like the stinging slugs which the Rio Kid had sent his way so, low over his new mount, he spurred for the narrows and disappeared.

A bullet burned Pryor's hand, stinging like a red-hot iron. The men stalking him were getting the range, and he would be unable to hold them off much longer. To jump down into the ravine would be certain death.

A huge boulder crashed on the lip of his protecting ledge, missed him by inches, and rolled on to strike heavily on the Cutoff floor. Gravel and smaller stones slid with it. The bandits had shoved it down, hoping to crush him.

"Hey, Frank, open up on that Rio Kid skunk!" shrieked an unseen Innocent from over his head. "He's right down below us!"

A dozen of the Innocents came toward the cliffs, and their guns rose to smash at the Rio Kid.

"Here we go!" Bob Pryor muttered grimly, snatching out a freshly loaded Colt.

When he first heard the bursts of gunfire

from above, he believed it was from the Innocents who were after him. Then he heard
them cursing in consternation, and one of
them, riddled with lead, hurtled past him
and landed with a dull thud in the canyon.

"Pryor! Captain Pryor!"

Sanders had finally arrived!

The Chief of the Vigilantes was leading
his fighting men to the rocks over the
Cutoff. Dismounted, for the going there was
too rough for horses, they surged in, rapidly
bringing up their carbines and Navy pistols.
The half dozen bandits seeking Pryor's life
were rapidly shot down.

Sanders' bearded face peered over the
brink at the Rio Kid.

"Where's Williams?" he shouted. "Is he all
right?"

"He's down to the right!" the Rio Kid
shouted back. "The whole mob's after him.
Open up on them skunks, Colonel!"

Sanders roared a command. His Vigilantes
let go, and four Innocents crashed from
their horses. The gang which had come
toward the Rio Kid felt the awful whoosh of
lead, and broke, most of them riding off to
the narrows.

Sanders called his followers. More and
more were leaping from their lathered,
muddy steeds and hurrying to join the fray.

They began working along the lip of the ravine, shooting into the back of the big gang of Innocents who had Captain Jim Williams and his men with his back to the wall. More of the bandits had appeared at the end of the Cutoff, to prevent any escape, and Williams had been forced to take to the rocks.

As Sanders brought his force to bear, their heavy fire ripped into the masked devils seeking Williams' life. Vigilante bullets cut down a dozen, wounding or killing, and the main band, realizing they were being ambushed in turn, spurred past the shooting troop with Jim Williams. Williams' men brought down three more of them before they escaped at the north end of the Cutoff.

The Rio Kid jumped down into the ravine, and ran to George Carter. He knelt by the gasping Confederate agent. Flecks of light-colored blood showed on Carter's lips.

"Carter!" the Rio Kid said. "I know yuh, and why yuh're here. I hoped to save yuh from Helm, but yore luck didn't hold."

"Doublecrossed me!" gasped Carter.

He was hit through the chest. Helm's bullet had cut between his ribs and torn a gaping hole as it emerged under his heart.

"They planned that all along," Bob Pryor said. "I heard 'em. . . . Here, have a drink.

. . . Plummer and Helm never meant to let yuh have that gold. The best yuh can do is take revenge. Where's that list of the Innocents yuh told Helm yuh had? Have yuh shore enough got one? They've got away, a good many of 'em. Our plans didn't work out the way we wanted 'em to, any more'n theirs did."

"Revenge — yeah, that's all — that's left! Who — who are yuh?"

"Remember the Confederate bummer at Robbers' Roost, Carter? Yuh're a smart man and a brave one. But I had to save the gold for my side, just as yuh hoped to get it for yores."

Carter's breath was rasping. He knew he had not much longer to live.

"Yuh'll — find the list — in the heel — left boot — hollow. So yuh're a spy, too."

He shuddered, raising his body up in a convulsion.

"Hurray — for Jeff Davis!" he whispered, and fell back.

Pity was in the Rio Kid's eyes as he looked down at the dead Confederate. He could understand. Carter had had a duty to perform, and he had died, trying to do it. Hat off, for moments he stood gazing down at George Carter, then knelt and began to remove the man's boot.

He had just found Carter's cache when he turned at the sound of a voice. Colonel Wilbur Sanders had come up.

"The devils!" growled Sanders, wiping the sweat and powder grime from his stern face. "Most of 'em escaped! The Chinook won for them, Pryor."

"Not altogether," replied the Rio Kid. "Take a peek at this, Colonel. I got it from Carter — or Major Smythe, as you knowed him. It's a full list of the Innocents, with Henry Plummer and Boone Helm leadin' the ball!"

"Let's see it!" cried Sanders eagerly.

He took the paper which the Rio Kid had extracted from the hollow heel of George Carter's boot. With narrowed eyes he read:

HENRY PLUMMER
BOONE HELM
NED RAY
BUCK STINSON
RED YAGER
SAMUEL BUNTON
HAYES LYONS

"They're all here," gloated Sanders.

They had driven the gang off Williams, who came from the rocks, his face damp with sweat. His blue eyes were dark with his fighting humor. Four of his men were wounded and one had died, but so skillfully had Williams handled his part that most of the party had escaped from the perilous trap with small damage.

He held out his big hand to the Rio Kid.

"Thanks," he said simply. "Yuh kept 'em from massacrin' us, Pryor."

"Shucks, let's get after that gold, 'fore Plummer and his bunch take it and run!" cried a Vigilante, one of the rank and file.

"We might catch up with Plummer," Sanders said. "Let's try."

The escaping Innocents had had horses under them. The Vigilantes had been forced to leave their worn, blown steeds up on the rim of the deep Cutoff. The outlaws had a long start and knew the mountains thoroughly. But, with the Rio Kid's list, obtained from the dead Confederate agent, George Carter, the Vigilantes could start picking up the bandits as they chose.

Half an hour later they had climbed back to the rim, leaving dead high-graders in the ravine, food for vulture and coyote. Williams was waiting for them at the south end of the cut, and the joined forces rode on the trail of the mule-train.

They found it two miles on, up a box canyon. The mules were unguarded and deserted and the packs had been broken open.

"Why, there ain't any gold in them!" gasped a bearded Vigilante. "Nothin' but sand!"

Sanders smiled grimly as he explained that the gold, safely cached in another spot in town, had been left with trusted guards.

"Only one box had a few gold bars on the top," he informed. "The rest were dummies, full of gravel, boys. We kept that from all but a few who were in the know. And Plummer soon found it out; he's a fox if ever there was one." Sanders' face was grave. "I only hope he goes back to Virginia City. But he may be too smart for that."

CHAPTER XX
CLEAN-UP

Men started back for Alder Gulch. The sun was up, and the Chinook was still blowing. The brown and red of the hills was beginning to show as the trails were cleared of snow. With astonishing speed, the hot breeze loosened winter's clutch. Little feeders that a horse usually could jump across had turned into raging torrents. And the riders returning to Virginia City, were slowed on the rough and rocky road.

"How about Robbers' Roost?" suggested the Rio Kid, as they hit the Gulch road and neared the side trail to the ridges. "We might find Boone Helm and some of his bunch there, Sanders."

Sanders nodded. "Come on, men. There's no sense in putting it off any longer."

He picked his men, and the Vigilantes rode.

In a little while the Rio Kid, scouting ahead, saw a dozen mustangs outside the saloon. He turned, waiting for Sanders to come up.

"Some of 'em in there," he reported.

Sanders gave terse commands. The Vigilantes spread out.

They circled, and the ring of grim, armed men began to close in on Robbers' Roost.

They must have been seen, for the front door opened and a man stepped out. Boone Helm stood there, his wounds bandaged, a sneer on his face as his eyes fixed on the approaching avengers. He turned toward his horse. But he saw a menacing ring of carbines pointing his way, and thought better of it.

As the Rio Kid and Sanders rode up, Helm snarled:

"Howdy, gents. What's up?"

"The jig is up, Helm," Pryor said coldly.

"Take his guns," Sanders ordered, in the same icy tone.

A red flash that was fear streaked through the desperado's terrible eyes. He licked his lips.

"I am innocent!" he cried.

"Watch them winders, Williams," cautioned the Rio Kid. "That's their password, callin' for help."

Jim Williams had already leaped from his horse. With gun drawn and backed by thirty of his men, he sprang to the door of Robbers' Roost. The Rio Kid pulled his Colt, to back him up. Bunched in the door were Helm's cronies, scowling, bearded bandits, ready for a fight.

Williams faced them. And when they met his eyes they hesitated, quailed, and did not show any fight.

Every man in that doorway was on Carter's list. And every man there was known as a murderer many times over.

"Guns off!" Williams ordered.

Helm was sneering at the Vigilante. Now he began to rail.

"Yuh got no right to do this! Yuh savvy that. Take me to Virginia City and I'll surrender to Sheriff Plummer."

"Forget Plummer," snapped Williams. "He can't help yuh now. Pass me that rope."

A silent miner handed Williams the knotted noose, and Williams tossed the other end over a handy oak limb.

"Anything to say?" asked Sanders. "Tell us the names of your friends, Helm."

Helm cursed him with vigorous fury, even as he faced his end. They waited until he was through.

"Your last request?" asked the colonel.

"Gimme a drink of whiskey."

A bottle was passed to him and Helm

drank long, smacked his lips.

"Never mind the blindfold," he snarled. "I'll jump."

Boone Helm climbed the crude ladder fetched from the barn.

"You're to blame for this, Sanders!" he shouted.

"Hurrah for Jeff Davis!"

He leaped, then. A minute later he was dead.

The others did not accept their fate so calmly. Several began groveling, begging for mercy. But when the grim Vigilantes rode from Robbers' Roost two hours later, on the trees dangled the killers of Alder Gulch. . . .

It was night when the avengers returned to Virginia City, and Henry Plummer was at home, in the house where he boarded.

Wilbur Sanders, James Williams, and the Rio Kid, backed by armed miners, approached the house.

"He's asleep," Plummer's landlady said when she came to the door, in answer to their summons.

They stepped toward the room she indicated, and on a couch saw the murderous, thieving sheriff. Muddy boots showed from under the couch. His stained coat, muddied by his swift ride, hung from a peg near at hand, and his six-shooters were suspended next to it.

He opened his eyes suddenly, and saw them standing near him.

"We want yuh to come with us, Plummer," Sanders said coldly.

Henry Plummer did not appear alarmed, although he guessed why they were there.

"Certainly," he agreed calmly. "I'll be with you as soon as I slip on my coat."

He rose, and started toward the pegs. The Rio Kid jumped over, standing close to the sheriff's guns. Plummer's left hand reached out, but he hesitated, then took down his hat and coat.

His moody eyes darted his hate at his arch-enemies, the Rio Kid, Williams and Sanders, then he was himself again, cool and collected.

They marched him to the outskirts of the town. A gallows — two long posts with a stout beam across the tops — was waiting. At sight of it, Plummer's nerve cracked.

"Sanders!" he gasped. "Can't you do anything about this?"

"Nothing, Plummer. You are to be hanged."

Henry Plummer, gunman and killer, road-agent, fiend behind his smooth, gentlemanly front, broke. He began to sob, begging for mercy.

"Don't hang me! Don't! Chain me forever if you want — banish me. Do anything, but don't hang me!"

The silent Vigilantes watched. They had two of Plummer's deputies, Ned Ray and Buck Stinson, waiting, under the same death sentence as the sheriff. Plummer fell on his knees, and screamed for mercy.

Ray and Stinson were pushed ahead toward the gallows.

"Bring up Plummer!"

The order given by the chief of the Vigilantes snapped like a pistol shot. Pryor and others started the sheriff forward, pulling him by the arms. He twisted from their grasp, and again groveled in the snow.

Then he seemed to gain some control. He stood up, walked to the scaffold and mounted the table beneath the gallows.

"Give me a good drop, men," he said. "That's a last favor."

The table was jerked from under him, and the fall broke his neck. Henry Plummer was dead. . . .

The Rio Kid stayed in Alder Gulch for another week, aiding Sanders and Williams in their thorough clean-up of the Innocents.

The word had gone out about the Montana Vigilantes' activities and evil characters were packing up to run for it. Some had confessed before they died, and given Sanders further assurance that the list which Bob Pryor had taken from George Carter, the Confederate spy, was correct.

Swift work by determined miner police bands had caught large numbers of the Innocents. Some escaped into the mountains, headed for tall timber, never to return, but many were caught, tried on the spot and hanged.

It was time for the Rio Kid to return to the Army, to his command. He knew that by the time he completed the long run back to the Eastern theater of the war, the wounds he had received in Montana would be healed. And his side was already strong enough for him to get back to Custer and his work as a scout.

He shook hands with Sanders and Williams, who would continue looking for scattered members of the broken Innocents.

"Sorry to see yuh go, Rio Kid," Jim Williams said, gripping his hand with the firmness of true friendship. "We could use yuh in these parts."

"We'll never forget the help you've given us," Sanders declared.

"Yuh'll see to it, then, that gold shipments

reach the Government mints safely?" asked Pryor.

"I'll make it my personal business, I promise."

"Good. Then I can ride back with a quiet mind, Colonel. Good-by, and good luck. Mebbe we'll meet again when the war's over."

The debonair Rio Kid strode out to where the groomed dun awaited him, with pack ready, carbine slung, clean and shining, under the saddle flap. Guns at his waist, Bob Pryor mounted and took the Gulch road out of Virginia City.

He followed its snakelike turnings, taking a final look at the dives and saloons, the wildness of the mining camps. The day was warming, for spring was at hand.

He turned off to Jefferson for a brief farewell. Young Adam Byrne came up from the diggings in the creek. The friends the Rio Kid had made gathered about him.

"I'm stayin' here, Bob," Byrne said eagerly.

He glanced toward Roberts' cabin, and the smile which Dorothy Roberts, standing there in the doorway, gave Byrne told the Rio Kid that for these two at least the bitterness of the war had ended.

General Roberts seized Bob Pryor's hand,

thanking him for all that he had done.

"Those scalawags got what they deserved, suh," he said gruffly. "I've heard of the gold business, Captain. Yuh've done what's right."

The Rio Kid shook hands all around. Then, mounting, he started for the Salt Lake Trail, the out-road, turning to smile and wave at the folks he had rescued from certain death at the hands of the terrible Innocents.

Apple blossoms were in bloom when he reached Washington. His name, taken in by an aide, brought him a quick audience with the President.

Abraham Lincoln gravely shook his hand, his eyes and mouth showing the strain he had been under throughout the Civil War. But things were going better, he told the Rio Kid.

"I've got a man named Grant in there, now," the President said. "He believes in winning, Captain."

"That's the only way, Mr. President."

He gave his report to Abraham Lincoln. The President thanked him. After a little more conversation the Rio Kid left, deeply flattered and pleased by the President's personal congratulations.

"With a man like him," he told himself gravely, "the Union's saved!"

It was the last time the brave scout was to look upon the great Emancipator, but Bob Pryor did not know that.

Forty-eight hours later he rejoined his command with Custer's brigade, taking up the war where he had left off. The Vigilantes of Montana were over two thousand miles away. It had been a perilous trail he had ridden with them — but the Rio Kid was to ride many a danger trail, once the war was done.

We hope you have enjoyed this Large Print book. Other Thorndike, Wheeler, and Chivers Press Large Print books are available at your library or directly from the publishers.

For information about current and upcoming titles, please call or write, without obligation, to:

Publisher
Thorndike Press
295 Kennedy Memorial Drive
Waterville, ME 04901
Tel. (800) 223-1244

or visit our Web site at:

www.gale.com/thorndike
www.gale.com/wheeler

OR

Chivers Large Print
published by BBC Audiobooks Ltd
St James House, The Square
Lower Bristol Road
Bath BA2 3SB
England
Tel. +44(0) 800 136919
email: bbcaudiobooks@bbc.co.uk
www.bbcaudiobooks.co.uk

All our Large Print titles are designed for easy reading, and all our books are made to last.